Sir Walter Besant

The Captains' Room

Vol. 1

Sir Walter Besant

The Captains' Room
Vol. 1

ISBN/EAN: 9783337082673

Printed in Europe, USA, Canada, Australia, Japan

Cover: Foto ©Andreas Hilbeck / pixelio.de

More available books at **www.hansebooks.com**

THE CAPTAINS' ROOM

ETC.

BY

WALTER BESANT

AUTHOR OF 'ALL SORTS AND CONDITIONS OF MEN' ETC.

IN THREE VOLUMES

VOL. I.

London

CHATTO & WINDUS, PICCADILLY

1883

LONDON : PRINTED BY
SPOTTISWOODE AND CO., NEW-STREET SQUARE
AND PARLIAMENT STREET

CONTENTS

OF

THE FIRST VOLUME.

THE CAPTAINS' ROOM.

CHAPTER I.

PAGE

THE MESSAGE OF THE MUTE . . 3

CHAPTER II.

THE PRIDE OF ROTHERHITHE 46

CHAPTER III.

THE SAILOR LAD FROM OVER THE SEA 67

CHAPTER IV.

OVERDUE AND POSTED . . . 109

CHAPTER V.

THE PATIENCE OF PENELOPE . 123

CHAPTER VI.

THE MESSAGE FROM THE SEA . 143

CHAPTER VII.

PAGE

Captain Borlinder among the Cannibals   171

CHAPTER VIII.

The Quest of Captain Wattles   .   .   201

CHAPTER IX.

The Great Good Luck of Captain Holstius   227

'LET NOTHING YOU DISMAY.'

CHAPTER I.

All the People Standing   .   271

THE CAPTAINS' ROOM

VOL. I.

CHAPTER I.

PERHAPS the most eventful day in the story of which I have to tell, was that on which the veil of doubt and misery which had hung before the eyes of Lal Rydquist for three long years was partly lifted. It was so eventful, that I venture to relate what happened on that day first of all, even though it tells half the story at the very beginning. That we need not care much to consider, because, although it is the story of a great calamity long dreaded and happily averted, it is a story of sorrow borne bravely, of faith, loyalty, and courage. A story such as one loves to tell, because, in the world of fiction, at least, virtue should always triumph, and true hearts be rewarded. Wherefore, if there be any who love to read of the mockeries of fate, the wasting of good women's love, the success of craft and treachery, instances of which are not wanting in the world, let them go elsewhere, or make a Christmas tale for themselves ; and their joy bells, if they like it,

shall be the funeral knell; and their noels a dirge
beside the grave of ruined and despairing innocence, and for their feast they may have the bread
and water of affliction.

The name of the girl of whom we are to
speak was Alicia Rydquist, called by all her friends
Lal; the place of her birth and home was a certain little-known suburb of London, called Rotherhithe. She was not at all an aristocratic person,
being nothing but the daughter of a Swedish
sea-captain and an English wife. Her father was
dead, and, after his death, the widow kept a
captains' boarding-house, which of late, for reasons which will presently appear, had greatly
risen in repute.

The day which opens my story, the day big
with fate, the day from which everything that
follows in Lal's life, whether that be short or long,
will be dated, was the fourteenth of October, in
the grievous year of rain and ruin, one thousand
eight hundred and seventy-nine. And though
the summer was that year clean forgotten, so that
there was no summer at all, but only the rain and
cold of a continual and ungracious April, yet
there were vouchsafed a few gracious days of
consolation in the autumn, whereof this was one,
in which the sun was as bright and warm as if he
had been doing his duty like a British sailor all
the summer long, and was proud of it, and meant

to go on giving joy to mankind until fog and gloom time, cloud and snow time, black frost and white frost time, short days and long nights time, should put a stop to his benevolent intentions.

At eleven o'clock in the forenoon, both the door and the window belonging to the kitchen of the last house of the row called 'Seven Houses' were standing open for the air and the sunshine.

As to the window, which had a warm south aspect, it looked upon a churchyard. A grape vine grew upon the side of the house, and some of its branches trailed across the upper panes, making a green drapery which was pleasant to look upon, though none of its leaves this year were able to grow to their usual generous amplitude, by reason of the ungenerous season. The churchyard itself was planted with planes, lime-trees, and elms, whose foliage, for the like reason, was not yellow, as is generally the case with such trees in mid-October, but was still green and sweet to look upon. The burying-ground was not venerable for antiquity, because it was less than a hundred years old, church and all; but yet it was pleasing and grateful—a churchyard which filled the mind with thoughts of rest and sleep, with pleasant dreams. Now, the new cemeteries must mostly be avoided, because one who considers them falls presently into grievous melancholy, which, unless diverted, produces insanity, suicide, or emigration. They lend a new and a horrid pang to death.

It is difficult to explain why this churchyard, more than others, is a pleasant spot: partly, perhaps, on account of the bright and cheerful look of the place in which it stands; then, there are not many graves in it, and these are mostly covered or honoured by grey tombstones, partly moss-grown. On this day the sunshine fell upon them gently, with intervals of shifting shade, through the branches; and though the place around was beset with noises, yet, as these were always the same, and never ceased except at night, they were not regarded by those who lived there, and so the churchyard seemed full of peace and quiet. The dead men who lie there are of that blameless race who venture themselves upon the unquiet ocean. The dead women are the wives of the men, their anxieties now over and done. When such men are gone, they are, for the most part, spoken of with good will, because they have never harmed any others but themselves, and have been kind-hearted to the weak. And so, from all these causes together, from the trees and the sunshine, and the memory of the dead sailors, it is a churchyard which suggested peaceful thoughts.

At all events it did not sadden the children when they came out from the school, built in one corner of it, nor did its presence ever disturb or sadden the mind of the girl who was making a pudding in the kitchen. There were sparrows in the branches, and in one tree sat a blackbird, now and then, late as it was, delivering himself of one note, just to remind himself of the past, and to keep his voice in practice against next spring.

The girl was fair to look upon, and, while she made her pudding, with sleeves turned back and flecks of white flour upon her white arms, and a white apron tied round her waist, stretching ·from chin to feet like a child's pinafore or a long bib, she sang snatches of songs, yet finished none of them; and when you come to look closer into her face you saw that her cheeks were thin and her eyes sorrowful, and that her lips trembled from time to time. Yet she was not thinking out her sad thoughts to their full capabilities of bitterness, as some women are wont to do—as, in fact, her own mother had done for close upon twenty years, and was still doing, having a like cause for plaint and lamentation ; only the sad thoughts came and went across her mind, as birds fly across a garden, while she continued deftly and swiftly to carry on her work.

At this house, which was none other than the well-known Captains' boarding-house, sometimes called 'Rydquist's, of Rotherhithe,' the puddings and pastry were her special and daily charge.

The making of puddings is the poetry of simple
cookery. One is born, not made, for puddings.
To make a pudding worthy of the name requires
not only that special gift of nature, a light and
cool hand, but also a clear intelligence and the
power of concentrated attention, a gift in itself, as
many lament when the sermon is over and they
remember none of it. If the thoughts wander,
even for a minute, the work is ruined. The in-
stinctive feeling of right proportion in the matter
of flour, lemon-peel, currants, sugar, allspice, eggs,
butter, breadcrumbs : the natural eye for colour,
form, and symmetry, which are required before
one can ever begin even to think of becoming a
maker of puddings, are all lost and thrown away,
unless the attention is fixed resolutely upon the
progress of the work. Now, there was one pudding, a certain kind of plum-duff, made by these
hands, the recollection of which was wont to fill
the hearts of those Captains who were privileged
to eat of it with tender yearnings whenever they
thought upon it, whether far away on southern
seas, or on the broad Pacific, or in the shallow
Baltic ; and it nerved their hearts when battling
with the gales, while yet a thousands knots at least
lay between their plunging bows and the Commercial Docks, to think that they were homeward
bound, and that Lal would greet them with that
pudding.

As the girl rolled her dough upon the white board and looked thoughtfully upon the little heaps of ingredients, she sang, as I have said, scraps of songs; but this was just as a man at work, as a carpenter at his bench or a cobbler over his boot, will whistle scraps of tunes, not because his mind is touched with the beauty of the melody, but because this little action relieves the tension of the brain for a moment, without diverting the attention or disturbing the current of thought. She was dressed—behind the big apron—in a cotton print, made up by her own hands, which were as clever with the needle as with the rolling-pin. It was a dress made of a sympathetic stuff—there are many such tissues in every draper's shop—which, on being cut out, sewn up, and converted into a feminine garment, immediately proceeds, of its own accord, to interpret and illustrate the character of its owner; so that for a shrew it becomes draggle-tailed, and for a lady careless of her figure, or conscious that it is no longer any use pretending to have a figure, it rolls itself up in unlovely folds, or becomes a miracle of flatness; and for a lady of prim temperament it arranges itself into stiff vertical lines; and for an old lady, if she is a nice old lady, it wrinkles itself into ten thousand lines, which cross and recross each other like the lines upon her dear old face, and all to bring her more respect and greater consideration ; but for a girl whose figure is tall and well-formed, this accommodating material becomes as clinging as the ivy, and its lines are every one of them an exact copy of Hogarth's line of beauty, due allowance being made for the radius of curvature.

I do not think I can give a better or clearer account of this maiden's dress, even if I were to say how-much-and-eleven-pence-three-farthings it was a yard and where it was bought. As for that, however, I am certain it came from Bjornsen's shop, where English is spoken, and where they have got in the window, not to be sold at any price, the greatest curiosity in the whole world (except the Golden Butterfly from Sacramento), namely, a beautiful model of a steamer, with everything complete—rigging, ropes, sails, funnel, and gear—the whole in a glass bottle. And if a man can tell how that steamer got into that bottle, which is a common glass bottle with a narrow neck, he is wiser than any of the scientific gentlemen who have tackled the problems of Stonehenge, the Pyramids, the Yucatan inscriptions, or the Etruscan language.

That is what she had on. As for herself, she was a tall girl ; her figure was slight and graceful, yet she was strong ; her waist measured just exactly the same number of inches as that of her grandmother Eve, whom she greatly resembled in beauty. Eve, as we cannot but believe, was the most lovely of women ever known, even including Rachel, Esther, Helen of Troy, Ayesha, and fair Bertha-with-the-big-feet. The colour of her hair depended a good deal upon the weather: when it was cloudy it was dark brown; when the sunlight fell upon it her hair was golden. There was quite enough of it to tie about her waist for a girdle, if she was so minded; and she was so little of a fine lady, that she would rather have had it brown in all weathers, and was half ashamed of its golden tint.

It soothes the heart to speak of a beautiful woman; the contemplation of one respectfully is, in itself, to all rightly constituted masculine minds, a splendid moral lesson.

'Here,' says the moralist to himself, 'is the greatest prize that the earth has to offer to the sons of Adam. One must make oneself worthy of such a prize: no one should possess a goddess who is not himself godlike.'

Having drawn his moral, the philosopher leaves off gazing, and returns, with a sigh, to his work. If you look too long, the moral is apt to evaporate and vanish away.

The door of the kitchen opened upon the garden, which was not broad, being only a few feet broader than the width of the house, but was long. It was planted with all manner of herbs, such as thyme, which is good for stuffing of veal;

mint, for seasoning of that delicious compound, and as sauce for the roasted lamb ; borage, which profligates and topers employ for claret-cup, though what it was here used for I know not ; parsley, good for garnish, which may also be chopped up small and fried ; cucumber, chiefly known at the West End in connection with salmon, but not disdained in the latitude of Rotherhithe for breakfast, dinner, tea, or supper, in combination with vinegar or anything else, for cucumber readily adapts itself to all palates save those set on edge with picksomeness. Then there were vegetables, such as onions, which make a noble return for the small space they occupy, and are universally admitted to be the most delightful of all roots that grow ; lettuces, crisp and green : the long lettuce and the round lettuce all the summer ; the scarlet-runner, which runneth in brave apparel, and eats short in the autumn, going well with leg of mutton ; and, at the end of the strip of ground, a small forest of Jerusalem artichoke, fit for the garden of the Queen. As for flowers, they were nearly over for the year, but there were trailing nasturtiums, long sprigs of faint mignonette, and one great bully hollyhock ; there were also, in boxes, painted green, creeping-jenny, bachelors'-button, thrift, ragged-robbin, stocks, and candy-tuft, but all over for the season. There was a cherry-tree trained against the wall, and beside it a peach ; there were also a Siberian crab, a medlar, and a mulberry-tree. A few raspberry canes were standing for show, because among them all there had not been that year enough fruit to fill a plate. The garden was separated from the churchyard by wooden pailings, painted green ; this made it look larger than if there had been a wall. It was, in fact, a garden in which not one inch of ground was wasted ; the paths were only six inches wide, and wherever a plant could be coaxed to grow, there it stood in its allotted space. The wall fruit was so carefully trained that there was not a stalk or shoot out of place ; the flower borders were so carefully trimmed that there was not a weed or a dead flower ; while as for grass, snails, slugs, bindweed, dandelion, broken flower-pot, brickbat, and other such things, which do too frequently disfigure the gardens of the more careless, it is delightful to record that there was not in this little slice of Eden so much as the appearance or suspicion of such a thing. The reason why it was so neat and so well watched was that it was the delight and paradise of the Captains, who, by their united efforts, made it as neat, snug, and orderly as one of their own cabins. There were live creatures in the garden, too. On half-a-dozen crossbars, painted green, were just so many parrots. They were all trained parrots, who could talk and did talk, not altogether as is the use of parrots, who too often give way to the selfishness of the old Adam, but one at a time, and deliberately, as if they were instructing mankind in some new and great truth, or delighting them with some fresh and striking poetical ejaculation. One would cough slowly, and then dash his buttons. If ladies were not in hearing he would remember other expressions savouring of fo'k'sle rather than of quarter-deck. Another would box the compass as if for an exercise in the art of navigation. Another seldom spoke except when his mistress came and stroked his feathers with her soft and dainty finger. The bird was growing old now, and his feathers were dropping out, and what this bird said you shall presently hear.

Next there was a great kangaroo hound, something under six feet high when he walked. Now he was lying asleep. Beside him was a little Maltese dog, white and curly; and in a corner—the warmest corner—there was an old and toothless bulldog. Other things there were—some in boxes, some in partial confinement, or by a string tied to one leg, some running about—such as tortoises, hedgehogs, Persian cats, Angola cats, lemurs, ferrets, Madagascar cats. But they were not all in the garden, some of them, including a mongoose and a flying-fox, having their abode on the roof, where they were tended faithfully by Captain

Zachariasen. In the kitchen, also, which was warm, there resided a chameleon.

Now, all these things—the parrots, the dogs, the cats, the lemurs, and the rest of them—were gifts and presents brought across the seas by amorous captains to be laid at the shrine of one Venus—of course I know that there never can be more than one Venus at a time to any well-regulated male mind—whom all wooed and none could win. There were many other gifts, but these were within doors, safely bestowed. It may also be remarked that Venus never refuses to accept offerings which are laid upon her altar with becoming reverence. Thus there were the fragile coral fingers, named after the goddess, from the Philippine Islands ; there were chests of the rich and fragrant tea which China grows for Russia. You cannot buy it at all here, and in Hong-Kong only as a favour, and at unheard-of prices. There were cups and saucers from Japan ; fans of the *coco de mer* from the Seychelles ; carved ivory boxes and sandal-wood boxes from China and India ; weapons of strange aspect from Malay islands ; idols from Ceylon ; praying tackle brought down to Calcutta by some wandering Thibetan ; with fans, glasses, mats, carpets, pictures, chairs, desks, tables, and even beds, from lands *d'outre mer*, insomuch that the house looked like a great museum or curiosity-shop. And everything, if you please, brought across the sea and presented by the original importers to the beautiful Alicia Rydquist, commonly called Lal by those who were her friends, and Miss Lal by those who wished to be, but were not, and had to remain outside, so to speak, and all going, in consequence, green with envy.

On this morning there were also in the garden two men. One of them was a very old man—so old that there was nothing left of him but was puckered and creased, and his face was like one of those too faithful maps which want to give every detail of the country, even the smallest. This was Captain Zachariasen, a Dane by birth, but since the age of eight on an English ship, so that he had clean forgotten his native language. He had been for very many years in the timber trade between the ports of Bergen and London. He was now, in the protracted evening of his days, enjoying an annuity purchased out of his savings. He resided constantly in the house, and was the dean, or oldest member among the boarders. He said himself sometimes that he was eighty-five, and sometimes he said he was ninety, but old age is apt to boast. One would not baulk him of a single year, and certainly he was very, very old.

This morning, he sat on a green box half-way down the garden—all the boxes, cages, railings, shutters, and doors of the house were painted a bright navy-green—with a hammer and nails in his hand, and sometimes he drove in a nail, but slowly and with consideration, as if noise and haste would confuse that nail's head, and make it go loose, like a screw. Between each tap he gazed around and smiled with pleased benevolence. The younger man, who was about thirty years of age, was weeding. That is, he said so. He had a spud with which to conduct that operation, but there were no weeds. He also had a pair of scissors, with which he cut off dead leaves. This was Captain Holstius, also of the mercantile marine, and a Norwegian. He was a smartly-dressed sailor—wore a blue cloth jacket, with trousers of the same; a red silk handkerchief was round his waist; his cap had a gold band round it, and a heavy steel chain guarded his watch. His face was kind to look upon. One noticed, especially, a greyish bloom upon a ruddy cheek. It was an oval face, such as you may see in far-off Bamborough, or on Holy Island, with blue eyes; and he had a gentle voice. One wonders whether the Normans, who so astonished the world a thousand years ago, were soft of speech, mild of eye, kind of heart, like their descendants. Were Bohemond, Robert the Devil, great Canute, like unto this gentle Captain Holstius? And if so, why were they so greatly feared? And if not, how is it that their sons have so greatly changed? They were sailors—the men of old. But sailors acquire an expression of unworldliness not found among us who have to battle with worldly and crafty men. They are not tempted to meet craft with craft, and treachery with deceit. They do not cheat; they are not tempted to cheat. Therefore, although the Vikings were ferocious and bloodthirsty pirates, thinking it but a small thing to land and spit a dozen Saxons or so, burn their homesteads, and carry away their pigs, yet, no doubt, in the domestic circle, they were mild and gentle, easily ruled by their wives, and obedient even to taking charge of the baby, which was the reason why they were called, in the pronunciation of the day, the hardy Nurse-men.

A remarkable thing about that garden was that if you looked to the north, over the garden walls of the Seven Houses, you obtained, through a kind of narrow lane, a glimpse of a narrow breadth of water, with houses on either side to make a frame. It was like a little strip of some panorama which never stops, because up and down the water there moved perpetually steamers, sailing-ships, barges, boats, and craft of all kinds. Then, if you turned completely round, and looked south, you saw, beyond the trees in the churchyard, a great assemblage of yard-arms, masts, ropes, hanging sails, and rigging. And from this quarter

there was heard continually the noise of labour
that ceaseth not—the labour of hammers, saws,
and hatchets ; the labour of lifting heavy burdens,
with the encouraging ‘ Yo-ho ’ ; the labour of men
who load ships and unload them ; the labour of
those who repair ships ; the ringing of bells which
call to labour ; the agitation which is caused in
the air when men are gathered together to work.
Yet the place, as has been already stated, was
peaceful.   The calm of the garden was equalled
by the repose of the open place on which the
windows of the house looked, and by the peace of
the churchyard.   The noise was without ; it
affected no one's nerves ; it was continuous, and,
therefore, was not felt any more than the ticking
of a watch or the beating of the pulse.

The old man presently laid down his hammer,
and spoke, saying, softly :

‘ Nor—wee—gee.’

‘ Ay, ay, Captain Zachariasen,’ replied the
other, pronouncing the name with a foreign
accent, and speaking a pure English, something
like a Welshman's English.   They both whispered,
because the kitchen door was open, and Lal might
hear.   But they were too far down the garden for
her to overhear their talk.

‘ Any luck this spell, lad ? ’

The old man spoke in a meaning way, with a
piping voice, and he winked both his eyes hard,

as if he was trying to stretch the wrinkles out of his face.

Captain Holstius replied, evasively, that he had not sought for luck, and, therefore, had no reason to complain of unsuccess.

'I mean, lad,' whispered the old man, 'have you spoke the barque which once we called the Saucy Lal? And if not '—because here the young man shook his head, while his rosy cheek showed a deeper red—' if not, why not?'

'Because,' said Captain Holstius, speaking slowly—' because I spoke her six months ago, and she told me ——'

Here he sighed heavily.

'What did she tell you, my lad? Did she say that she wanted to be carried off and married, whether she liked it or not?'

'No, she did not.'

'That was my way, when I was young. I always carried 'em off. I married 'em first and axed 'em afterwards. Sixty year ago, that was. Ay, nigh upon seventy, which makes it the more comfortable a thing for a man in his old age to remember.'

'Lal tells me that she will wait five years more before she gives him up, and even then she will marry no one, but put on mourning, and go in widow's weeds—being not even a wife.'

'Five years!' said Captain Zachariasen. ' 'Tis

a long time for a woman to wait for a man. Five
years will take the bloom off of her pretty cheeks,
and the plumpness off of her lines, which is now
in the height of their curliness. Five years to
wait! Why, there won't be a smile left on her
rosy lips. Whereas, if you'd the heart of a
loblolly boy, Cap'en Holstius, you'd ha' run her
round to the church long ago, spoke to the clerk,
whistled for the parson, while she was still occupied with the pudding and had her thoughts far
away, and—well, there, in five years' time she'd
be playin' with a four-year-old, or maybe twins,
as happy as if there hadn't never been no Cap'en
Armiger at all.'

'Five years,' Captain Holstius echoed, 'is a
long time to wait. But any man would wait
longer than that for Lal, even if he did not get
her, after all.'

'Five years! It will be eight, counting
the three she has already waited for her dead
sweetheart. No woman, in the old days, was
ever expected to cry more than one. Not in my
day. No woman ever waited for me, nor dropped
one tear, for more than one twelvemonth, sixty
years ago, when I was dr——' Here he recollected that he could never have been drowned, so
far back as his memory served. That experience
had been denied him. He stopped short.

'She thinks of him,' Captain Holstius went on,

seating himself on another box, face to face with the old man, 'all day; she dreams of him all night; there is no moment that he is not in her thought—I know because I have watched her; she does not speak of him: even if she sings at her work, her heart is always sad.'

'Poor Rex Armiger! Poor Rex Armiger!' This was the voice of the old parrot, who lifted his beak, repeated his cry, and then subsided.

Captain Holstius's eyes grew soft and humid, for he was a tender-hearted Norwegian, and he pitied as well as loved the girl.

'Poor Rex Armiger!' he echoed; 'his parrot remembers him.'

'She is wrong,' said the old man, 'very wrong. I always tell her so. Fretting has been known to make the pastry heavy: tears spoil gravy.' He stated this great truth as if it was a well-known maxim, taken from the Book of Proverbs.

'That was the third time that I spoke to her; the third time that she gave me the same reply. Shall I tease her more? No. Captain Zachariasen, I have had my answer, and I know my duty.'

'It's hard, my lad, for a sailor to bear. Why, you may be dead in two years, let alone five. Most likely you will. You look as if you will. What with rocks at sea and sharks on land, most sailors, even skippers, by thirty years of age, is nummore. And though some '—here he tried to

recollect the words of Scripture, and only succeeded in part—' by good seamanship escape, and
live to seventy and eighty, or even, as in my case,
by a judgmatic course and fair winds, come to
eighty-five and three months last Sunday, yet in
their latter days there is but little headway, the
craft lying always in the doldrums, and the rations,
too, often short. Five years is long for Lal to
wait in suspense, poor girl! Take and go and
find another girl, therefore,' the old man ad-
vised.

'No'—the Norwegian shook his head sadly—
' there is only one woman in all the world for
me.'

'Why, there, there,' the old Captain cried,
' what are young fellows coming to? To cry after
one woman! I've given you my advice, my lad,
which is good advice; likely to be beneficial to
the boarders, especially them which are per-
manent, because the sooner the trouble is over,
the better it'll be for meals. I did hear there
was a bad egg, yesterday. To think of Rydquist's
coming to bad eggs! But if a gal will go on
fretting after young fellows that is long since food
for crabs, what are we to expect but bad eggs?
Marry her, my lad, or sheer off, and marry some
one else. P'raps, when you are out of the way,
never to come back again, she will take on with
some other chap.'

Captain Holstius shook his head again.

'If Lal, after three years of waiting, says she cannot get him out of her heart—why, why there will be nothing to do, no help, because she knows best what is in her heart, and I would not that she married me out of pity.'

'Come to pity!' said Captain Zachariasen, 'she can't marry you all out of pity. There's Cap'en Borlinder and Cap'en Wattles, good mariners both, also after her. Should you like her to marry them out of pity?'

'I need not think of marriage at all,' said the Norwegian. 'I think of Lal's happiness. If it will be happier for her to marry me, or Captain Borlinder, or Captain Wattles, or any other man, I hope that she will marry that man; and if she will be happier in remembering her dead lover, I hope that she will remain without a husband. All should be as she may most desire.'

Then the girl herself suddenly appeared in the doorway, shading her eyes from the sunshine, a pretty picture, with the flour still upon her arms, and her white bib still tied round her.

'It is time for your morning beer, Captain Zachariasen,' she said. 'Will you have it in the kitchen, or shall I bring it to you in the garden?'

'I will take my beer, Lal,' replied the old man, getting up from the box, 'by the kitchen fire.'

He slowly rose and walked, being much bent and bowed by the weight of his years, to the kitchen door.

Captain Holstius followed him.

There was a wooden armchair beside the fire, which was bright and large, for the accommodation of a great piece of veal already hung before it. The old man sat down in it, and took the glass of ale, cool, sparkling, and foaming, from Lal's hand.

'Thoughtful child,' he said, holding it up to the light, ' she forgets nothing—except what she ought most to forget.'

'You are pale to-day, Lal,' said the Norwegian, gently. 'Will you come with me upon the river this afternoon ? '

She shook her head sadly.

'Have you forgotten what day this is, of all days in the year ? ' she asked.

Captain Holstius made no reply.

'This day, three years ago, I got his last letter. It was four months since he sailed away. Ah me ! I stood upon the steps of Lavender Dock and saw his ship slowly coming down the river. Can I ever forget it ? Then I jumped into the boat and pulled out mid-stream, and he saw me and waved his handkerchief. And that was the last I saw of Rex. This day, three years and four months ago, and at this very time, in the forenoon.'

The old man, who had drained his glass and was feeling just a little evanescent headiness, began to prattle in his armchair, not having listened to their talk.

'I am eighty-five and three months, last Sunday; and this is beautiful beer, Lal, my dear. 'Twill be hard upon a man to leave such a tap. With the Cap'ens' room; and you, my Lal.'

'Don't think of such things, Captain Zachariasen,' cried Lal, wiping away the tear which had risen in sympathy for her own sorrows, not for his.

' 'Tis best not,' he replied, cheerfully. ' Veal, I see. Roast veal! Be large-handed with the seasonin', Lal. And beans? Ah! and apple-dumplings. The credit of Rydquist's must be kept up. Remember that, Lal. Wherefore, awake, my soul, and with the sun. Things there are that should be forgotten. I am eighty-five and a quarter last Sunday, like Abraham, Isaac, and Jacob—even Methusalem was eighty-five once, when he was little more than a boy, and never a grey hair—and, like the patriarchs at their best and oldest, I have gotten wisdom. Then, listen. Do I, being of this great age, remember the gals that I have loved, and the gals who have loved me? No. Yet are they all gone like that young man of yourn, gone away and past like gales across the sea. They are gone, and I am hearty. I shall never see them nummore ; yet I sit down regular to meals, and still play a steady knife and fork. And what I say is this : "Lal, my dear, wipe them pretty eyes with your best silk pockethandkercher, put on your best frock, and go to church in it for to be married." '

'Thank you, Captain Zachariasen,' said the girl, not pertly, but with a quiet dignity.

'Do not,' the old man went on—his eyes kept dropping, and his words rambled a little— 'do not listen to Nick Borlinder. He sings a good song, and he shakes a good leg. Yet he is a rover. I was once myself a rover.'

She made no reply. He yawned slowly and went on :

'He thinks, he does, as no woman can resist him. I used to have the same persuasion, and I found it sustaining in a friendly port.'

'I do not suppose,' said Lal, softly, 'that I shall listen to Captain Borlinder.'

'Next,' the old man continued, ' there is Cap'en Wattles. Don't listen to Wattles, my dear. It is not that he is a Yankee, because a Cap'en is a Cap'en, no matter what his country, and I was, myself, once a Dane, when a boy, nigh upon eighty years ago, and drank corn brandy, very likely, though I have forgotten that time, and cannot now away with it. Wattles is a smart seaman ; but Wattles, my dear, wouldn't make you happy. You want a cheerful lad, but no drinker and toper like Borlinder ; nor so quiet and grave as Wattles, which isn't natural, afloat nor ashore, and means the devil.'

Here he yawned again and his eyes closed.

' Very good, sir,' said Lal.

' Yes, my dear—yes—and this is a very—comfortable—chair.'

His head fell back. The old man was asleep.

Then Captain Holstius drew a chair to the kitchen door, and sat down, saying nothing, not looking at Lal, yet with the air of one who was watching over and protecting her.

And Lal sat beside the row of freshly-made dumplings, and rested her head upon her hands, and gazed out into the churchyard.

Presently her eyes filled with tears, and one of them in each eye overflowed and rolled down her cheeks. And the same phenomenon might have been witnessed directly afterwards in the eyes of the sympathetic Norweegee.

It was very quiet, except, of course, for the screaming of the steam-engines on the river, and the hammering, yo-ho-ing, and bell-ringing of the Commercial Docks ; and these, which never ceased, were never regarded. Therefore, the calm was as the calm of a Sabbath in some Galilean village, and broken only in the kitchen by the ticking of the roasting-jack, and an occasional remark made, in a low tone, by a parrot.

Captain Holstius said nothing. He stayed there because he felt, in his considerate way, that his presence soothed and, in some sort, comforted the girl. It cost him little to sit there doing nothing at all.

Of all men that get their bread by labour it is the sailor alone who can be perfectly happy doing nothing for long hours together. He does not even want to whittle a stick.

As for us restless landsmen, we must be continually talking, reading, walking, fishing, shooting, rowing, smoking tobacco, or in some other way wearing out brain and muscle.

The sailor, for his part, sits down and lets time run on, unaided. He is accustomed to the roll of his ship and the gentle swish of the waves through which she sails. At sea he sits so for hours, while the breeze blows steady and the sails want no alteration.

So passed half an hour.

While they were thus sitting in silence, Lal suddenly lifted her head, and held up her finger, saying, softly,

'Hush! I hear a step.'

The duller ears of her companion heard nothing but the usual sounds, which included the trampling of many feet afar off.

' What step ? ' he asked.

Her cheeks were gone suddenly quite white and a strange look was in her eyes.

' Not his,' she said. ' Oh, not the step of my Rex ; but I know it well for all that. The step of one who —— Ah ! listen ! '

Then, indeed, Captain Holstius became aware of a light hesitating step. It halted at the open door (which always stood open for the convenience of the Captains), and entered the narrow hall. It was a light step, for it was the step of a barefooted man.

Then the kitchen door was opened softly, and Lal sprang forward, crying, madly :

' Where is he ? Where is he ? Oh, he is not dead ! '

At the sound of the girl's cry the whole sleepy place sprang into life ; the dogs woke up and ran about, barking with an immense show of alertness, exactly as if the enemy was in force without the walls ; the Persian cat, which ought to have known better, made one leap to the palings, on which she stood with arched back and upright tail, looking unutterable rage ; and the parrots all screamed together.

When the noise subsided, the new comer stood in the doorway. Lal was holding both his hands, crying and sobbing.

Outside, the old parrot repeated :

'Poor Rex Armiger! Poor Rex Armiger!'

Captain Zachariasen, roused from his morning nap, was looking about him, wondering what had happened.

Captain Holstius stood waiting to see what was going to happen.

The man, who was short in stature, not more than five feet three, wore a rough cloth sailor's cap, and was barefoot. He was dressed in a jacket, below which he wore a kind of petticoat, called, I believe, by his countrymen, who ought to know their own language, a 'sarong' His skin was a copper colour; his eyes dark brown; his face was square, with high cheek-bones; his eyes were soft, full, and black; his mouth was large with thick lips; his nose was short and small, with flat nostrils; his hair was black and coarse—all these characteristics stamped him as a Malay.

Captain Zachariasen rubbed his eyes.

'Ghosts ashore!' he murmured. 'Ghost of Deaf-and-Dumb Dick!'

'Who is Dick?' answered Captain Holstius.

'Captain Armiger's steward—same as was drowned aboard the Philippine three years ago along with his master and all hands. Never, nevermore heard of, and he's come back.'

The Malay man shook his head slowly. He kept on shaking it, to show them that he quite understood what was meant, although he heard no word.

'Where is he? Oh, where is he?' cried the girl again.

Then the dumb man looked in her face and smiled. He smiled and nodded, and smiled again.

'Like a Chinaman in an image,' said Captain Zachariasen. 'He can't be a ghost at the stroke of noon. That's not Christian ways nor Malay manners'

But the smile, to Lal, was like the first cool draught of water to the thirsty tongue of a wanderer in the desert. Could he have smiled were Rex lying in his grave?

A Malay who is deaf and dumb is, I suppose, as ignorant of his native language as of English; but there is an atmosphere of Malayan abroad in his native village out of which this poor fellow picked a language of his own. That is to say, he was such a master of gesture as in this cold land of self-restraint would be impossible.

He nodded and smiled again. Then he laughed aloud, meaning his most cheerful note; but the laughter of those who can neither hear nor speak is a gruesome thing.

Then Lal, with shaking fingers, took from her bosom a locket, which she opened and showed the man. It contained, of course, the portrait of her lover.

He took it, recognised it, caught her by one hand, and then, smiling still, pointed with eyes that looked afar towards the east.

'Lies buried in the Indian Ocean,' murmured the old man ; 'I always said it.'

Lal heard him not. She fell upon the man's neck and embraced and kissed him.

'He is not dead,' she cried. 'You hear, Captain Holstius? Oh, my friend, Rex is not dead. I knew he could not be dead—I have felt that he was alive all this weary time. Oh, faithful Dick !' She patted the man's cheek and head as if he was a child. 'Oh, good and faithful Dick ! what shall we give him as the reward for the glad tidings ? We can give him nothing—nothing—only our gratitude and our love.'

' And dinner, may be,' said Captain Zachariasen. 'No, not the veal, my dear ; ' for the girl, in her hurry to do something for this messenger of good tidings, made as if she would sacrifice the joint. 'First, because underdone veal is unwholesome even for deaf and dumb Malays ; second, roast veal is not for the likes of him, but for Cap'ens. That knuckle of cold pork now——'

Lal brought him food quickly, and he ate, being clearly hungry.

' Does he understand English ? ' asked Captain Holstius.

'He is deaf and dumb ; he understands nothing.'

When he had broken bread, Dick stood again, and touched the girl's arm, which was equivalent to saying, ' Listen, all of you!'

The man stood before them in the middle of the room with the open kitchen door behind him, and the sunlight shining upon him through the kitchen window. And then he began to act, after the fashion of that Roman mime, who was able to convey a whole story with by-play, under-plot, comic talk, epigrams, tears, and joyful surprises, without one word of speech. The gestures of this Malay were, as I have said, a language by themselves. Some of them, however, like hieroglyphics before the Rosetta Stone, wanted a key.

The man's face was exceedingly mobile and full of quickness. He kept his eyes upon the girl, regarding the two men not at all.

And this, in substance, was what he did. It was not all, because there were hundreds of little things, every one of which had its meaning in his own mind, but which were unintelligible, save by Lal, who followed him with feverish eagerness and attention. Words are feeble things at their best, and cannot describe these swift changes of face and attitude.

First, he retreated to the door, then leaped with a bound into the room. Arrived there he looked about him a little, folded his arms, and began to walk backwards and forwards, over a length of six feet.

'Come aboard, sir,' said Captain Zachariasen, greatly interested and interpreting for the benefit of all. 'This is good mummicking, this is.'

Then he began to jerk his hand over his shoulder each time he stopped. And he stood half-way between the extremities of his six-foot walk and lifted his head as one who watches the sky. At the same time Lal remarked how by some trick of the facial muscles, he had changed his own face. His features became regular, his eyes intent and thoughtful, and in his attitude he was no longer himself, but—in appearance—Rex Armiger.

'They're clever at mummicking and conjuring,' said Captain Zachariasen; 'I've seen them long ago, in Calcutta, when I was in—— '

'Hush!' cried Lal imperatively. 'Do not speak! Do not interrupt.'

The Malay changed his face and attitude, and was no more Rex Armiger, but himself; then he held out his two hands, side by side, horizontally, and moved them gently from left to right and right to left, with an easy wave-like motion, and at the same time he swung himself slowly backwards and forwards. It seemed to the girl to imitate the motion of a ship with a steady breeze in smooth water.

'Go on,' she cried; 'l understand what you mean.'

The man heard nothing, but he saw that she followed him, and he smiled and nodded his head.

He became once more Rex Armiger. He walked with folded arms, he looked about him as one who commands and who has the responsibility of the ship upon his mind.

Presently he lay down upon the floor, stretched out his legs straight, and with his head upon his hands went to sleep.

'Even the skipper's bunk is but a narrow one,' observed Captain Zachariasen, to show that he was following the story, and proposed to be the principal interpreter.

The dumb actor's slumber lasted but a few moments. Then he sprang to his feet and began to stagger about. He stamped, he groaned, he put his hand to his head, he ran backwards and forwards; he presented the appearance of a man startled by some accident; he waved his arms, gesticulated wildly, put his hands to his mouth as one who shouts.

Then he became a man who fought, who was dragged, who threatened, who was struck, tramping all the while with his feet so as to produce the impression of a crowd.

Then he sat down and appeared to be waiting, and he rocked to and fro continually.

Next he went through a series of pantomimic exercises which were extremely perplexing, for he strove with his hands as one who strives with a rope, and he made as one who is going hand over hand, now up, now down a rope; and he ran to and fro, but within narrow limits, and presently he sat down again, and nodded his head and made signs as if he were communicating with a companion.

'Dinner-time,' said Captain Zachariasen, 'or, may be, supper.'

After awhile, still sitting, he made as if he held something in his hand which he agitated with a regular motion.

'Rocking the baby,' said Captain Zachariasen, now feeling his way surely.

Lal, gazing intently, paid no heed to this interruption.

Then he waved a handkerchief.

'Aha!' cried Captain Zachariasen; 'I always did that myself.'

Then he lay down and rested his head again upon his arm; but Lal noticed that now he curled up his legs, and the tears came into her eyes, because she saw that he, personating her Rex, seemed for a moment to despair.

But he sat up again, and renewed that movement, as if with a stick, which had made the old skipper think of babies.

Then he stopped again, and let both arms drop to his side, still sitting.

'Tired,' said Captain Zachariasen. 'Pipe smoke time.'

The Malay did not, however, make any show of smoking a pipe. He sat a long time without moving, arms and head hanging.

Then he started, as if he recollected something suddenly, and taking paper from his pocket, began to write. Then he went through the motion of drinking, rolled up the paper very small, and did something with it difficult to understand.

'Sends her a letter,' said the Patriarch, nodding his head sagaciously. 'I always wrote them one letter after I'd gone away, so's to let 'em down easy.'

This done, the Malay seated himself again, and remained sitting some time. At intervals he lay down, his head upon his hands as before, and his legs curled.

The last time he did this he lay for a long time—fully five minutes—clearly intending to convey the idea of a considerable duration of time.

When he sat up, he rubbed his eyes and looked about him. He made motions of surprise and joy, and, as before, communicated something to a companion. Then he seemed to grasp something, and began again the same regular movement, but with feverish haste, and painfully, as if exhausted.

'Baby again!' said the wise man. 'Rum thing to bring the baby with him.'

Then the Malay stopped suddenly, sprang to his feet, and made as if he jumped from one place to another.

Instantly he began again to rush about, shake and be shaken by shoulders, arms, and hands, to stagger, to wave his hands, finally to run along with his hands straight down his sides.

'Now I'm sorry to see this,' said Captain Zachariasen mournfully. 'What's he done? Has that baby brought him into trouble? Character gone for life, no doubt.'

Lal gazed with burning eyes.

Then the Malay stood still, and made signs as if he were speaking, but still with his arms straight to his sides. While he spoke, one arm was freed, and then the other. He stretched them out as if for relief. After this, he sat down, and ate and drank eagerly.

'Skilly and cold water,' said Captain Zachariasen. 'Poor young man!'

Then he walked about, going through a variety of motions, but all of a cheerful and active character. Then he suddenly dropped the personation of Rex Armiger, and became himself again.

Once more he went through that very remarkable performance of stamping, fighting, and drag-
ging.

Then he suddenly stopped and smiled at Lal.
The pantomime was finished.

The three spectators looked at each other en-
quiringly, but Lal's face was full of joy.

'I read this mummicking,' said Captain Zachariasen, 'very clearly, and if, my dear, without
prejudice to the dumplings, which I perceive to
be already finished, and if I may have a pipe,
which is, I know, against the rules in the kitchen
—but so is a mouthing mummicking Malay—I
think I can reel you off the whole story, just as
he meant to tell it, as easy as I could read a ship's
signals.　Not that every man could do it, mind
you ; but being, as one may say, at my oldest and
best——'

Lal nodded.　Her eyes were so bright, her
cheeks so rosy, that you would have thought her
another woman.

'Go, fetch him his pipe, Captain Holstius,' she
said.　Then, seized by a sudden impulse, she
caught him by both hands.　'It could never have
been,' she said, ' even—even—if—— You will
rejoice with me ? '

'If it is as you think,' he said, ' I both rejoice
and thank the Father humbly.'

Fortified with his pipe, the old man spoke

slowly, in full enjoyment of his amazing and patriarchal wisdom.

'Before Cap'en Armiger left Calcutta,' he began, 'he did a thing which many sailors do, and when I was a young man, now between seventy and eighty years ago, which is a long time to look back upon, they always did. Pecker up, Lal, my beauty. You saw how the mummicker rolled his eyes, smacked his lips, and clucked his tongue. Not having my experience, prob'ly you didn't quite understand what he was wishful for to convey. That meant love, Lal, my dear. Those were the signs of courting, common among sailors. Your sweetheart fell in love with you in the Port of London, and presently afterwards with another pretty woman in the Port of Calcutta, which is generally the way with poor Tom Bowling. She was a snuff-and-butter, because at Calcutta they are as plenty as blackberries; and when young, snuff-and-butter is not to be despised, having bright eyes; and there was another thing about her which I guess you missed, if you got so far as a right understanding of the beginning. She was a widow. How do I know she was a widow? This way. The mummicking Malay, whose antics can only be truly read, like the signs of the weather, by the wisdom of eighty and odd, put his two hands together. You both saw that—second husband that meant. Then he waved his hands up and down. If I rightly make out that signal it's a signal of distress. She led the poor lad, after he married her, a devil of a life. Temper, my girl, goes with snuff-and-butter, though when they're young I can't say but there's handsome ones among them. A devil of a life it was, while the stormy winds did blow, and naturally Cap'en Armiger began to cast about for to cut adrift.'

'Go on, Captain Zachariasen,' said Lal, who only laughed at this charge of infidelity.

The Malay looked on gravely, understanding no word, but nodding his head as if it was all right.

'He marries this artful widow then, and, in due course, he has a baby. You might ha' seen, if you'd got my eyes, which can't be looked for at your age, that the mummicking mouther kept rocking that baby. Very well, then; time passes on, he has a row with the mother; she, as you may have seen, shies the furniture at his head, which he dodges, being too much of a man and a sailor to heave the tables back. Twice she shies the furniture. Then he ups and off to sea, taking —which I confess I cannot understand, for no sailor to my knowledge ever did such a thing before—actually taking—the—baby—with him!' The sagacious old man stopped, and smoked a few moments in meditation. 'As to the next course in this voyage,' he said, ' I am a little in doubt. For whether there was a mutiny on board, or whether his last wife followed him and carried on shameful before the crew, whereby the authority of the skipper was despised and his dignity lowered, I cannot tell. Then came chucking overboards, and whether it was Cap'en Armiger chucking his wife and baby, or whether he chucked the crew, or whether the crew chucked him, is not apparent, because the mummicker mixed up Jonah and the crew, and no man, not even Solomon himself, in his cedar-palace, could tell from his actions which was crew and which was Jonah. However, the end is easy to understand. The Cap'en, in fact, was run in when he got to shore—you all saw him jump ashore—for this chucking overboard, likely. He made a fight for it, but what is one man against fifty. So they took him off, with his arms tied to his sides, being a determined young fellow, and he was tried for bigamy, or chucking overboard, or some such lawful and statutable crime. And he was then sentenced to penal servitude for twenty years or it may be less. At Brisbane, Queensland, it was, perhaps, or Sydney, New South Wales, or Singapore, or perhaps Hong-Kong, I can't say which, because the mummicker at this point grew confused. But it must be one of these places where there's a prison. There he is still, comfortably

working it out. Wherefore, Lal, my dear, you
may go about and boast that you always knew he
was alive, because right you are and proud you
may be. At the same time, you may now give
up all thoughts of that young chap, and turn
your attentions, my dear, to'—here he pointed
with his pipe—' to the Norweegee.'

Captain Holstius, who had shaken his head a
.great deal during the Seer's interpretation, shook
his head again, deprecatingly.

'Thank you, Captain Zachariasen,' said Lal,
laughing. What a thing joy is! She laughed.
who had not laughed for three years. The
dimples came back to her cheek, the light to her
eyes. 'Thank you. Your story is a very likely
one, and does your wisdom great credit. Shall I
read you my interpretation of this acting?'

The Captain nodded.

'Rex set sail from Calcutta with a fair wind,
leaving no wife behind, and taking with him no
baby. How long he was at sea I know not;
then there came a sudden storm, or perhaps the
striking on a rock, or some disaster. Then he is
in an open boat alone with Dick here, though
what became of the crew I do not know; then
he writes me a letter, but I do not understand
what he did with it when he had written it; then
they sit together expectant of death; they row
aimlessly from time to time; they have no provi-

sions ; they suffer greatly ; they see land, and they row as hard as they can ; they are seized by savages and threatened, and he is there still among them. He is there, my Rex, he is there, waiting for us to rescue him. And God has sent us this poor dumb fellow to tell us of his safety.'

The old man shook his head.

'Poor thing ! ' he said compassionately. 'Better enquire at every British port, where there's a prison, in the East, after an English officer working out his time, and ask what he done, and why he done it ? '

' Let be, let be,' said Captain Holstius. ' Lal is always right. Captain Armiger is among the savages, somewhere. We will bring him back. Lal, courage, my dear ; we will bring him back to you alive and well ! '

CHAPTER II.

THE PRIDE OF ROTHERHITHE.

THE terrace or row called Seven Houses is situated, as I have stated above, in a riverside township, which, although within sight of London Bridge, is now as much forgotten and little known as any of the dead cities on the Zuyder-Zee or the Gulf of Lyons. In all respects it is as quiet, as primitive, and as little visited, except by those who come and go in the matter of daily business.

The natives of Rotherhithe are by their natural position, aided by the artificial help of science, entirely secluded and cut off from the outer world. They know almost as little of London as a Highlander or a Cornish fisherman. And as they know not its pleasures, they are not tempted to seek them ; as their occupations keep them for the most part close to their own homes, they seldom wander afield ; and as they are a people contented and complete in themselves, dwelling as securely and with as much satisfaction as the men of Laish, they do not desire the society of strangers. Therefore great London, with its noises and mighty business, its press and hurry, is a place which they care not often to encounter; and as for the excitement and amusements of the West, they know them not. Few there are in Rotherhithe who have been farther west than London Bridge, fewer still who know the country and the people who dwell west of Temple Bar.

It is a place protected and defended, so to speak, by a narrow pass, or entrance, uninviting and unpromising, bounded by river on one side and docks on the other. This Thermopylæ passed, one finds oneself in a strange and curious street with water on the left and water on the right, and ships everywhere in sight.

It possesses no railway, no cabstand, no omnibus runs thither; there is no tram. The nearest station is for one end, Thames Tunnel, and for the other, Deptford. All the local arrangements for getting from one place to the other seem based on the good old principle that nobody wants to get from one place to the other; one would not be astonished to meet a string of pack-horses laden with the produce of the town, so quiet, so still, so far removed from London, so old-world in its aspect is the High Street of Rotherhithe.

If, however, they are little interested in the great city near which they live, they know a great deal about foreign countries and strange climates; if they have no politics, they read and talk much about the prospects of trade across the sea; they do not take in 'Telegraph,' 'Standard,' or 'Daily News,' but they read from end to end that admirable paper the 'Shipping and Mercantile Gazette.' For all their prospects and all their interests are bound up in the mercantile marine. No one lives here who is not interested in the Commercial Docks, or the ships which use them, or the boats, or in the repairs of ships, or in the supply of ships, or in the manners, customs, and requirements of skippers, mates, and mercantile sailors of all countries. Their greatest man is the Superintendent of the Docks, and after him, in point of importance, are the dock-masters and their assistants.

Rotherhithe consists, for the most part, of one long street, which runs along the narrow strip of ground left between the river and the docks when they were built. The part of the river thus overlooked is Limehouse Reach; the street begins at the new Thames Tunnel Station, which is close beside the old Rotherhithe Parish Church, and it ends where Deptford begins. There are many beautiful, and many wonderful, and many curious streets in London 'and her daughters;' but this is, perhaps, the most curious. It is, to begin with, a street which seems to have been laid down so as to get as much as possible out of the way of the ships which press upon it to north and south. Ships stick their bows almost across the road, the figure-heads staring impertinently into first-floor windows. If you pass a small court or wynd, of which there are many, with little green-shuttered houses, you see ships at the end of it, with sails hanging loosely from the yard-arms.

On the left hand you pass a row of dry docks. They are all exactly alike; they are built to accommodate one vessel, but rarely more; if you look in, no one questions your right of entrance; and if you see one you have seen them all.

Look, for instance, into this dry dock. Within her is a two-masted sailing vessel; most likely she hails from Norway or from Canada, and is engaged in the timber trade. Her planks show signs of age, and she is shored up by great round timbers like bits of a mast. Her repairs are probably being executed by one man, who is seated on a hanging board leisurely brandishing a paint-brush. Two more men are seated on the wharf, looking on with intelligent curiosity. One man—perhaps the owner of the ship, or some other person in authority—stands at the far end of the dock and surveys the craft with interest, but no appearance of hurry, because the timber trade, in all its branches, is a leisurely business.

No one is on board the ship except a dog, who sits on the quarter-deck sound asleep, with his nose in his paws.

The wharf is littered all about with round shores, old masts, and logs of ship timber; it is never tidied up, chips and shavings lie about rotting in the rain, the remains of old repairs long since done and paid for, upon ships long since gone to the bottom; there is a furnace for boiling pitch, and barrels for the reception of that useful article; there is a winch with rusty chains; there is a crane, but the wheels are rusty. The litter and leisure of the place are picturesque. One wonders who is its proprietor; probably some old gentleman with a Ramillies wig, laced ruffles, gold buckles on his shoes, silk stockings, a flowered satin waistcoat down to his knees, sober brown coat, and a gold-headed stick.

At the entrance to the dock there is a little house with green shutters, a pretence of green railings which enclose three feet of ground, and green boxes furnished with creeping-jenny and mignonette. But this cannot be the residence of the master.

Beyond the dock, kept out by great gates which seem not to have been opened for generations, so rusty are the wheels and so green are their planks with weed and water-moss, run the waters of the Thames. There go before us the steamers, the great ocean steamers, coming out of the St. Katherine's, London, and West India Docks ; there go the sailing ships, dropping easily down with the tide, or slowly making way with a favourable breeze up to the Pool ; there creep the lighters and barges, heavily laden, with tall mast and piled-up cargo, the delight of painters ; there toil continually the noisy steam-tug and the river packet steamer ; there play before us unceasingly the life, the movement, the bustle of the Port of London.

But all this movement, this bustle, seems to us, standing in the quiet dock, like a play, a procession of painted ships upon a painted river, with a background of Limehouse church and town all most beautifully represented ; for the contrast is so strange.

Here we are back in the last century ; this old ship, whose battered sides the one man is tinkering, is a hundred years old ; the Swedish skipper, who stands and looks at her all day long, in no hurry to get her finished and ready for sea, flourished before the French Revolution ; the same leisurely dock, the same leisurely carpenter, the same leisurely spectators, the same green palings, the same little lodge with its green door and green flower-box, were all here a hundred years ago and more ; and we, who look about us, find ourselves presently fumbling about our heads to see whether, haply, we wear tye-wigs and three-cornered hats.

On the doors of this dock we observe an announcement warning marine-store dealers not to enter. What have they done—the marine-store dealers?

A little farther on there is another dry dock. We look in. The same ship, apparently; the same leisurely contemplation of the ship by the same man; the same dog; the same contrast between the press and hurry of the river and the leisure of the dock; the same warning to marine-dealers. Again we ask, what have they done—the marine-store dealers?

Some of the docks have got suggestive and appropriate names. The 'Lavender' leads the poet to think of the tender care bestowed upon ships laid up in that dock (the name is not an advertisement, but a truthful and modest statement); the 'Pageant' is magnificent; the 'Globe' suggests geographical possibilities which cannot but fire the imagination of Rotherhithe boys; and what could be more comfortable for a heart of oak than 'Acorn' Wharf?

One observes presently a strange sweet fragrance in the air, which, at first, is unaccountable. The smell means timber. For behind the street lie the great timber docks. Here is timber stacked in piles; here are ships unloading timber; here is timber lying in the water. It is timber from Canada and from Norway; timber from Honduras; timber from Singapore; timber from every country where there are trees to cut and hands to cut them.

It is amid these stocks of timber, among these ships, among these docks, that the houses and gardens of Rotherhithe lie embowered.

Some of the houses were built in the time of great George Tertius. One recognises the paucity of windows, the flat façade, the carved, painted, and varnished woodwork over the doors. More, however, belong to his illustrious grandfather's period, or even earlier, and some, which want painting badly, are built of wood and have red-tiled roofs.

Wherever they can they stick up wooden palings painted green. They plant scarlet-runners wherever they can find so much as a spare yard of earth. They are fond of convolvulus, mignonette, and candy-tuft in boxes. They all hammer on their walls tin plates, which show to those who can understand that the house is insured in the 'Beacon.' And some of the houses—namely, the oldest and smallest—have their floors below the level of the street.

There is one great house — only one — in Rotherhithe. It was built somewhere in the last century, before the Commercial Docks were excavated.   It was then the home of a rich merchant living among the dry docks—probably he was the proprietor of Lavender and Acorn Docks. There is a courtyard before it; the door, with a porch, stands at the top of broad stairs ; there is ornamental stone-work half-way up the front of the house ; and there is a gate of hammered iron, as fine as any in South Kensington.

The shops have strange names over the doors. They are chiefly kept by Norwegians, Dutchmen, Swedes, and Danes, with a sprinkling of Rotherhithe natives.   The things exhibited for sale look foreign.   Yet we observe with satisfaction that the public-houses are kept by Englishmen, and that the Scandinavian taste in liquor is catholic. They can drink—these Northmen—and do, anything which ' bites.'

Quite at the end of this long street you come to a kind of open place, in which stands the terrace called ' Seven Houses.'   They occupy the east side.   On the west is, first, a timber-yard, open to the river; next a row of houses, white, neat, and clean ; beyond the terrace is the church, with its churchyard and schools.   Then there is another short street, with shops, the fashionable shopping-place of Rotherhithe.   And here the town, properly so called, ends, for beyond is the entrance to the Commercial Docks, and all around spread great sheets of water, in which lie the timber-ships from Norway, Sweden, Canada, Archangel, Stettin, Memel, Dantzic, St. Petersburgh, Savannah, and the East.

Hither, too, come ships from New Zealand, bringing grain and wool, and here put in ships, but in smaller number, bound for almost every port upon the globe.

And what with the green trees in the church-yard, the clean houses, the bright open space, the ships in the dock, and the glimpses of the river, one might fancy oneself not in London at all, but across the North Sea and in Amsterdam.

It was in Rotherhithe that Lal Rydquist was born, and in Rotherhithe she was educated. Nor for eighteen years and more did the girl ever go outside her native place, but continued as ignorant of the great city near her as if it did not exist. On the other hand, from the conversation of those around her, she became perfectly familiar with the greater part of the globe; namely, its oceans, seas, ports, harbours, gulfs, bays, currents, tides, prevalent winds, and occasional storms. Most people are brought up to know nothing but the land: it is shameful favouritism to devote geography books exclusively to the land upon this round globe; Lal knew nothing about the land, but a good deal about the water. Such other knowledge as she had acquired pertained to ships, harbours, cargoes, Custom dues, harbour dues, bills of lading, insurance, wet and dry docks, and the current price of timber, grain, rice, and so forth. A very varied and curious collection of facts lay stored in her brain; but as for the accomplishments and acquirements of ordinary English girls, she knew none of them.

Her christian-name was Alicia. When she was but a toddler, the sailor folk with whom she played, and who gave her dolls, called her Lal. As she grew up, these honest people remained her friends, and therefore her name remained. Girls grow up, by Nature's provision, gradually, so that there never comes a time when a pet name ceases of its own accord. Therefore, to the Captains, who used the boarding-house, being all personal friends,—none but friends, in fact, were admitted to the privileges of that little family hotel—she continued to be Lal.

The boarding-house was carried on by Mrs. Rydquist, Lal's mother, who had been a notable woman in her day. The older inhabitants of Rotherhithe testified to that effect. But her misfortunes greatly affected and changed her for the worse. One need only touch upon the drowning of her father, which happened many years before, and was regarded by the burgesses of Rotherhithe as a special mercy bestowed upon his family, so wasteful was he and fond of drink when ashore. He was chief officer of an East Indiaman which went down with all hands in a cyclone, as was generally believed, somewhere north of the Andaman Islands, outward bound. He had spent all his pay in ardent drinks, and there was nothing left for his daughter. But she married a stout fellow, a Swede by nation, and Rydquist by name, who sailed to and fro between the ports of Bjorneborg and London, Captain and part owner of a brig in the timber trade. Alas! that brig dropped down stream one morning as usual, having the captain on board, and leaving the captain's wife ashore with the baby, and she was never afterwards heard of. Also there was some trouble about the insurance, and so the captain's widow got nothing for her husband's share in the ship.

Mrs. Rydquist, then a young woman and comely still, who might have married again, took to crying, and continued to cry, which was bad for the boarding-house which her husband's friends started for her. In most cases time cures the deadliest wounds, but in this poor lady's case the years went on and she continued to bewail her misfortunes, sitting, always with a tea-pot before her, upon a sofa as hard as a bed of penitence, and plenty of pocket-handkerchiefs in her lap.

There could not have been a happier child, a brighter, merrier child, a more sunshiny child, a more affectionate child, a more contented child than Lal, during her childhood, but for two things.

Her mother was always crying, and the house went on anyhow. When she grew to understand things a little, she ventured to point out to her mother that men who go to sea do often get drowned, and among the changes and chances of this mortal life, this accident must be seriously considered by the woman who marries a sailor. But no use. She remonstrated again, but with small effect, that the house was not kept with the neatness desired by captains; that it was in all respects ill-found; that the quality of the provisions was far from what it ought to be, and that meals were not punctual. The aggravation of these things, and the knowledge that they were received with muttered grumblings by the good fellows who put up with them chiefly for her own sake, sank deep into her heart, and shortened— not her life, but her schooling.

When she was fourteen, being as tall and shapely as many a girl of eighteen, she would go to school no more. She announced her intention of staying at home; she took over the basket of keys — that emblem of authority — from her mother's keeping into her own; she began to order things; she became the mistress of the house, while the widow contentedly sat in the front parlour and wept, or else, which made her deservedly popular among the captains, prophesied, to anyone who would listen, shipwreck, death, and ruin, like Cassandra, Nostradamus, and Old Mother Shipton, to these friends.

Immediately upon this assumption of authority the house began to look clean, the windows bright, the bedrooms neat; immediately the enemies of the house, who were the butcher, the baker, the bacon-man, the butterman, and every other man who had shot expensive rubbish into the place, began, to use the dignified language of the historian, to 'roll back sullenly across the frontier.' Immediately meals became punctual; immediately rules began to be laid down and enforced. Captains must henceforth only smoke in the evening; captains must pay up every Saturday; captains must not bring friends to drink away the rosy hours with them; captains must moderate their language—words beginning with a D were to be overhauled, so to speak, before use; captains must complain to Lal if they wanted anything, not go about grumbling with each other in a mean and a mutinous spirit. These rules were not written, but announced by Lal herself in peremptory tones, so that those who heard knew that there was no choice but to obey.

She was the best and kindest of managers; she made such a boarding-house for her captains as was never dreamed of by any of them. Such dinners, such beer, spirits of such purity and.

strength, tobacco of the finest; no trouble, no disturbance, the wheels always running smoothly. Captains' bills made out to a penny, with no surcharge or extortion. And, withal, the girl was thoughtful for each man, mindful of what he liked the best, and with a mother's eye to buttons.

It was indeed a boarding-house fit for the gods. So startling were the 'effects' in cleanliness that honest Dutchmen rubbed their eyes, and seeing the ships all round them, thought of the Boompjes of Rotterdam; not a plank in the house but was like a tablecloth for cleanliness.

Then, as to punctuality: at the stroke of eight, breakfast on the table, and Lal, neat as a bandbox, pouring out tea and coffee, made as they should be; while toast, dry and buttered, muffins, chops and steaks, ham and eggs, bacon, and fish just out of the frying-pan, were on the table.

On the stroke of one, the dinner, devised, planned, and personally conducted by Lal, herself, more diligently than any cook of modern or ancient history, was borne from the kitchen to the Captains' room.

The nautical appetite is large, both on shore and afloat; but on shore it is critical as well. The skipper aboard his ship may contentedly eat his way through barrels of salt junk, yet ashore he craves variety, and is as particular about his vegetables as a hippopotamus who has studied the art of dining.

And this is the reason, not generally understood, why the market-gardens in the neighbourhood of Deptford are so extensive, and why every available square inch of Rotherhithe grows a cabbage or a scarlet-runner.

There were no complaints here, however, about vegetables.

Tea was served at five, for those who wanted any.

Supper appeared at eight; and after supper, grog and pipes. Yet, as at dinner the supply of beer was generous yet not wasteful, so at night, every captain knew that if he wanted more than his ration, or double ration, he must get up and slink out of the house like a truant school-boy, to seek it at the nearest public-house.

The mercantile skipper in every nation is much the same. He is a responsible person, somewhat grave; ashore he does not condescend to high jinks, and leaves sprees to the youngsters. Yet among his fellows in such a house as Rydquist's, he is not above a song or even a cheerful hornpipe. He is generally a married man with a large family of whom he is fond and proud. He reads little, but has generally some book to talk of; and he is brimful of stories, mostly, it must be owned, of a professional and pointless kind, and some old,

old Joe Millers, which he brings out with an air
as if they were new and sparkling from the mint
of fancy.

These men were the girl's friends, all the
friends she had. They were fond of her and
kind to her. When, as often happened, she found
herself in the Captains' room in the evening and
sat on the arm of Captain Zachariasen's chair, the
stories went on with the songs and the laughing,
just as if she was not present, for they were an
innocent-minded race, and whether they hailed
from Russia, Sweden, Norway, Denmark, Holland,
or America, they were chivalrous and respected
innocence.

The house accommodated no more than half-a-
dozen, but it was always full, and the captains
were of the better sort. Captain Hansen from
Christiania dropped in after his ship was in dock ;
if the house was full he went back to his ship ; if
he could have a room he stayed there. The same
with Captain Bebbington of Quebec, Captain
Griggs of Edinburgh, Captain Rosenlund of
Hamburg, Captain Eriksen of Copenhagen,
Captain Vidovich of Archangel, Captain Ling of
Stockholm, and Captain Tilly of New Brunswick,
and a dozen more.

They rallied round Rydquist's ; they thought
it a proud thing to be able to put up there ; and
they swore by Lal.

Then who but Lal overhauled the linen, gave out some to be mended and some to be condemned, and rigged them out for the next voyage? And as for confidences, the girl was not fifteen years old before she knew all the secrets of all the men who went there, with their love stories, their disappointments, their money matters, their hopes, and their ambitions. And she was already capable, at that early age, of giving sensible advice, especially in matters of the heart. Those who followed that advice subsequently rejoiced: those who did not, repented.

When she was seventeen, they all began, with one consent, to fall in love with her. She remarked nothing unusual for awhile, having her mind greatly occupied in considering the price of vegetables, which during that year remained like runagates for scarceness. Presently, however, the altered carriage of the boarders was impossible to be otherwise than remarkable.

Love, we know, shows itself by many external symptoms. Some went careless of attire; some went in great bravery with waistcoats and neckties difficult to describe and impossible to match; some laughed, some heaved sighs, some sang songs; one or two made verses; those who were getting grey tried to look as if they were five-and-twenty, and made as if they still could shake a rollicking leg; those who were already turned of sixty persuaded themselves that a master mariner's heart is always young, and that no time of life is too far advanced for him to be a desirable husband.

Lal laughed and went on making the puddings ; she knew very well what they wanted, but she felt no fancy, yet, for any of them.

When, which speedily happened, one after the other came to lay themselves, their ships, and their fortunes at her feet, she sent them all away, not with scorn or unkindness, but with a cheerful laugh, bidding them go seek prettier, richer, and better girls to marry ; because, for her own part, she had got her work to do, and had no time to think about such things, and if she had ever so much time she most certainly would not marry that particular suitor.

They went away, and for a while looked gloomy and ashamed, fearing that the girl would tell of them. But she did not, and they presently recovered, and when their time came and their ships were ready, they dropped down the river with a show of cheerfulness, and so away to distant lands, round that headland known as the Isle of Dogs, with no bitterness in their hearts, but only a little disappointment, and the most friendly feelings towards the girl who said them nay.

When these were gone, the house, which was

never empty, received another batch of Captains, old and young. Presently similar symptoms were developed with them ; all were ardent, all confident. They had been away a year or two. They found the little Lal, whom they left a handy maiden, a mere well-grown girl of fourteen or so, developed into a tall and beautiful young woman. Upon her shoulders, invisible to all, sat Love, discharging arrows right and left into the hearts of the most inflammable of men. This batch—excepting two, who had wives in other ports, and openly lamented the fact—behaved in the same surprising manner as their predecessors. They were presently treated with the same dismissal, but with less courtesy, because to the girl this behaviour was becoming monotonous, and it sometimes seemed as if the whole of mankind had taken leave of their senses. They retired in their turn, and when their ships were laden, they, too, sailed away a little discomfited, but not revengeful or bearing malice. Then came a third batch, and so on. But of sea-captains there is an end : Lal's friends one after the other, came, disappeared after a while, and then came back again. Those who used the house at Rotherhithe where like comets rather than planets, because they had no fixed periods, but returned at intervals which could only be approximately guessed. When, however, the cycle was fulfilled, and there was no more to fall in love with her (strangers, as has been stated, not being admitted), there was a lull, and the rejected, when they came back again and found the girl yet heart free, rejoiced, because every man immediately became confident that sooner or later Lal's fancy would fall upon him ; and every man cherished in his own mind the most delightful anticipations of a magnificent wedding feast, with the joy of Rotherhithe for the bride, and himself for bridegroom.

CHAPTER III.

THE SAILOR LAD FROM OVER THE SEA.

A WOMAN'S fate comes to her, like most good or bad things, unexpectedly. Nothing is sure, says the French proverb, but the unforeseen. Nothing could have been more unexpected, for instance, than that the falling overboard of a Malay steward from an Indian liner should have led to the sorrow and the happiness of Lal Rydquist. That this was so you will presently read, and the fact suggests a fine peg for meditation on causes and effects. Had it not been for that event, this story, which it is a great joy to write, would never have been written, and mankind would have been losers to so great an extent; whereas, that temporary immersion in the cold waters of the river in Limehouse Reach produced so many things one after the other that they have now left Lal in the possession of the most necessary ingredient of happiness quintessential. We all know what that is, and in so simple a matter a lifting of the eye is as good as a printer's sheet of words.

And could one, had it not been so, have had the heart to write this tale? Why, instead of a Christmas story, it would have been a mere winter's tale, a Middle-of-March story, a searching, biting, east-wind story, fit only to be cut up and gummed upon doors and windows to keep out the cold.

When the dinner was off her mind, served, commended, and eaten, and when her mother was deposited for the day upon the sofa, with tea-pot and the kettle ready, the pocket-handkerchiefs for weeping, the book which she never read in, and, perhaps, one of the younger Captains who had not yet heard the story of her misfortunes more than a dozen times or so; or with some of her friends among the widows and matrons of Rotherhithe, with whom she would exchange prophecies of disasters, general and particular; Lal would hasten to enjoy herself after her free and independent fashion. One of the Captains had given her a little dingy, and taught her how to row it, and her pleasure was to paddle about the river in Limehouse Reach, dodging the steamers, and watching the craft as they went up and down.

This is a pursuit full of peril, because steamers in ballast sometimes come down the river at a reckless speed, their pilots being drunk, cutting down whatever falls in their way; yet to a girl who is handy with her sculls, and has a quick eye, the danger is part of the delight. On the Thames in Limehouse Reach one may be easily run over and one's boat cut in two. There then follows a bad time for a few moments, while the victim of the collision is getting drowned or saved; still, if one thinks of danger, half the fun of the world is gone. Lal thought of the change, the amusement, the excitement: on the Thames there is continual life, movement, and activity; on the Thames, there may be found by girls, sometimes worried by perpetual housekeeping, rest and soothing. As for Lal, the daily press of work was practically finished with the dinner, because the 'service' might be trusted with the rest. And after dinner, on the river she breathed fresh air. Here was not only mental rest, but also exercise for her young muscles; here was all the amusement and variety she ever desired; here she could even let her imagination wander abroad, to the pinnacles and spires of the city of which she knew so little even by hearsay, or to the foreign lands of which she heard so much. Above all, she was alone. This is so rare, so unattainable a thing to most girls, even to those who do not make puddings for sea-captains, that one quite understands how Lal valued the privilege. Her life was all before her. Like other maidens she loved to sit by herself and take a Pisgah-like view of her future. It might lie among the steeples and streets—she had never heard of any West End splendours—of London; it might be in those far-off lands where some of her Captains had wives; say, in New Brunswick, or beside the beauty of the Great St. Lawrence, or even in Calcutta, or in Dantzic, or in Norway; or it might lie always in simple and secluded Rotherhithe, among the timber piles of the Commercial Docks. Not a girl given to self-communings, tearing her religion up by the roots to see how it was getting on, or the doubts which nowadays seem to assail most fiercely those who have the least power or knowledge to help them to a solution, a quiet, simple, cheerful, hopeful girl, with a smile for everyone and a laugh for all her friends, yet a girl so hard-worked and so full of responsibilities that there were days when she had what the French ladies call an attack of nerves, and must fain get away from all and float at rest, thinking of other things than the wickedness of butchers, upon the bosom of the great river.

Sometimes, if the weather was too rough for her little boat, she would paddle along the bank till she came to the mouth of the Commercial Docks, and there would row about among the timber ships, watching the men at work, and the great planks being shot from the portholes in the stern of the vessels, or the dockmen piling the timbers, or the foreign sailors idling about upon the wharves. But mostly she loved the river.

Now it came to pass, one Saturday afternoon late in the month of May, and the year eighteen hundred and seventy-six, that Lal happened to be out in her boat upon the river. It was a delightful afternoon, quite an old-fashioned May day, without a breath of east wind, a sky covered with light flying clouds, so that the sunshine dropped about in changing breadths, now here and now there, throwing a bright patch upon the water, gilding a steeple, flashing from a window, making even a stumpy little tug glorious for a moment. She sang to herself as she sat in her boat, not a loud song like a Siren or a Lurlei person, but a gentle happy melody—I think it was some hymn —and she sat with her face to the bows, keeping the boat's head well to the waves raised by the swell of the passing ships. She was quite safe herself, being near the shore and between two heavily-laden lighters, waiting for tide to go up stream; the river was rising, and was covered with all kinds of craft.

Presently she became aware of a vast great ship, one of the big Indian liners, slowly rounding the Isle of Dogs. A great ship always attracted her imagination; it is a thing so vast, so easily moved, and so life-like. As the tall hull drew nearer, her eyes were fixed upon it, and she paddled a little beyond her protecting lighters, so as to get a better view of the vessel as she passed.

The ship moved up stream slowly here, because the river was so full. First Lal saw from her place the lofty bows, straight cut like a razor, rounding the Isle of Dogs and steadily growing nearer. Then her pilot put her a point more to starboard, and Lal saw the long and lofty side of her, her portholes open wide, high out of the water. Along the bulwarks were ranged a line of faces, mostly pale with Indian summers, but not all; they were the faces of the passengers who leaned over and watched the crowded river and talked together. Lal wondered whether they were glad to come home again, and what they were telling each other, and she hoped they would think their country improved since they saw it last; and then ventured in mute wish to congratulate their mothers, daughters, and sisters, wives, sweethearts, and all female cousins, relatives, and friends, that the ship had not gone to Davy's Locker on her homeward voyage, with so many brave fellows on board. The ship belonged to the great Indian Peninsular Line, and was called the " Aryan." She was so great a ship, and she moved so slowly, that Lal had time for a great many observations as she passed her. Also when her little boat was about midships, still kept bows-on to meet the coming-waves, one of the passengers, a young fellow, took off his hat to her with a loud ' Hurrah ! ' He meant a respectful salutation to the first pretty girl they had met in the good old country, which is full of the prettiest girls in the world. Lal wondered what it felt like, this coming home. All her life long she had been among men who went out of port and presently put into port again ; one or two, in her own experience, never came back, having met with the fate reserved for many sailors ; but that was not a home-coming like that of these exiles from India. There would be joy in their homes, no doubt, but what would the poor fellows themselves feel after these years of separation ? The feminine mind, everybody knows very well, reserves nearly all its sympathies for the sufferings of the men ; while it is an honourable trait in the male character, that it is roused to fury by the sufferings of women.

Just before the ship passed her, the great wave which rolled upwards from her keel came curling six feet high, like the Bore of the Severn and the Parrott, towards Lal's little boat. The lighters reeled and rolled, she seized her sculls and held her bows straight, steady to meet the swell, so that the little vessel gallantly rode over the wave ; and this passed swiftly on trying to swamp everything in its way, and presently capsized a boat with two promising and ambitious young thieves, who had gone down the river gaily, hoping to pick up plunder by the way. They got no plunder on that occasion, but a wet skin and a very near escape from the habitual criminal life for which they were preparing themselves. In this they are now, in fact, actively engaged; insomuch that one has been in prison during three of the five years since that event, and the other two and a half years. When they are out they enjoy themselves very much and drink bad gin. Then the wave caught a Greenwich steamboat and knocked the land-lubber passengers off their legs; and then it filled and sunk a barge full of hay. The hay went down the river with the next tide and littered the shore of Greenwich, where people who went down to dine gazed upon it from the windows of the Ship. There was also a sister or a brother wave on the north bank, proceeding from the starboard bow, but I do not know what mischief that wave succeeded in accomplishing.

While Lal was considering the ways of this swell, and looking to see what a pother, with a rolling and a rocking and a staggering to and fro it caused, she heard a sudden splash, and right in front of her she was aware of a man in the water. Immediately afterwards another man leaped gallantly from the ship after the first man, and a moment afterwards came up to the surface holding him.

Then, without waiting to think, because at such moments the reasoning faculty only brings people to grief and discredit, Lal shot her boat ahead to help, for certainly the two appeared to want immediate assistance, and that so badly, that if it came not at once, they would very soon want it no longer. Their arms were interlocked, they beat, or one of them beat, the water helplessly; their heads kept disappearing and coming up again. On the ship there was a crowd of faces, terror-stricken. The girl caught one hand as her boat came to the spot. The hand belonged to one of the two men, that was clear, but whether the first or the second she could not tell; in fact, only that one hand and a little piece of coat cuff were at the moment visible above water, and probably the next moment there would have been nothing at all. The fingers clutched hers like a vice. Lal threw herself down in the boat to prevent being drawn over, and caught the wrist with her other hand.

Then the group, so to speak, emerged again from the water, and the hand the girl had seized caught the gunwale of the boat, and the eyes in the head which belonged to the hand opened, and the mouth in the head gasped something inarticulate. As for the man's other hand and the whole of the rest of him, that was locked tight in the embrace of the first man who had fallen overboard. It is, anybody knows, the general custom and the base ingratitude of persons who are drowning, to try and drown their rescuers.

'Row us ashore quickly,' cried the one who clung to the gunwale; 'I can hold on for a spell. He won't let go, even to be helped into the boat.'

The ship was brought to now, and there was a vast crowd of passengers, and the officers shouting and gesticulating.

They saw the action of the girl in the boat, and then they saw her seize the sculls and pull vigorously to shore. · As for Lal, all she saw was a pale and dripping face, fingers which clutched the gunwale and nearly pulled it under, and an indiscriminate something in the water.

'Oh, can you hold on?' she cried. 'It is but a moment—twenty strokes—see, we are close to the steps.'

'Quick!' he replied; 'it is a heavy weight. Row as hard as you can, please.'

Presently, when the captain of the ship saw the boat landed at the steps, and was sure of the safety of the two men, he made a sign to the pilot, and the ship went on her way, for time is precious.

'Lucky escape,' he said. 'Armiger will come over presently, none the worse for a ducking.'

But the passengers with one accord raised a mighty cheer as the boat touched the shore, and the men on the lighters cheered lustily, and even the two young capsized thieves, who were wet and dripping, cheered. And there were some who said the case must be forwarded to the Royal Humane Society; and some who talked about Grace Darling, and made comparisons; and some who said it was their sacred duty to write to the papers, and tell the story of this wonderful presence of mind. But they did not, because shortly afterwards they reached the docks, and there was kissing of relations, packing of wraps, counting of boxes, and afterwards so much to see and talk about, and so many things to tell, that the rescue of the second officer in the Thames became only an incident in the history of the voyage, and the voyage itself only an incident in the history of their sojourn abroad.

The distance to be rowed was more, indeed, than twenty strokes, but not much more. Still, there are times when twenty strokes of the oar take more time, to the imagination, than many hours of ordinary work. Lal rowed with beating heart; in two minutes the boat lay alongside the steps.

When her passenger's feet touched the stones he let go, and, being a strong young fellow, and none the worse for his cold bath, he carried his burden, an apparently inanimate body, up the stairs to the top. Here he laid him while he ran down again to help his preserver.

'These are my steps,' she said; 'my boat is

always moored here. Thank you, but if you don't give her the whole length of her painter she will be hung up by the bows when the tide runs out.'

She jumped out and ran lightly up the stone steps. At the top the man who had given them all this trouble sat up, looking about him with wondering eyes. Then Lal saw that he was of some foreign country, partly by his dress and partly from his face. The other, who did indeed present a rueful appearance in his dripping clothes, was, she perceived, an officer of the steamer. Then Lal began to laugh.

'It is all very well to laugh,' he said, grimly, and shaking himself like Tommy Trout, medallist of the Humane Society, after rescuing that Tom, ' but here's half my kit ruined. And, I say, you've saved my life and I haven't even thanked you. But I do not know how to thank you.'

' It was all by chance,' replied Lal, 'and I am very glad.'

' And what are we to do next?' he asked.

He made a sign to the other man, who sprang to his feet, shivered, and nodded.

'I am very glad you saved his life, at any rate,' the young man went on ; ' he is the steward of the officers' mess, and he cannot thank you himself, because he is deaf and dumb; we call him Dick.'

'Come, both of you,' said the girl, recovering her wits, which were a little scattered by this singular event. 'Come, both, and dry your clothes.'

She led the way, and they all three set off running—a remarkable procession of one dry girl and two wet men, which drew all eyes upon them, and a small following of boys, in the direction of the Captains' house.

'I thought we should have dragged the gun-wale under water,' gasped the young fellow.

'So did I,' said Lal, simply. 'Can you swim?'

'No,' he replied.

'Yet you jumped overboard to rescue your steward. What a splendid thing to do.'

'I forgot I couldn't swim till I was in the water. Never mind. I mean to learn.'

The young fellow was a tall, slight-built lad of twenty-one or twenty-two. Lal pushed him into a bedroom, and pointed to a bundle of clothes. It was not her fault that they belonged to Captain Jansen, who was five feet nothing high, and about the same round the waist. So that when the lad was dressed in them he felt a certain amount of embarrassment, as anyone might who was sent forth into an unknown house with trousers no longer than his knees, and of breadth phenomenal.

'Where can I hide,' he said to himself, 'till the things are dry?'

He found a room set with a long table and a

good many chairs. This was the Captains' room, where they took their meals by day and smoked pipes at night. Just then no one was in it. He wanted to find the girl who had saved his life and rescued him ; so, after a look round, he went on his cruise of discovery.

Next, he opened another door. It was Lal's housekeeping room, in which sat an old, old man in an armchair, sound asleep. This was Captain Zachariasen.

He shut the door quietly and opened another. This was the front parlour, and in it sat Mrs. Rydquist alone, also fast asleep ; but the opening of the door awakened her, and she sat up and put on her spectacles.

'Come in, Captain,' she said, thinking it was one of her friends, but uncertain which of them looked so young and wore clothes of such an amplitude. 'Come in, Captain. It is a long time since we have had a talk.'

'Thank you, ma'am,' he replied. 'It is my first visit here. We always, you know, put into East India Docks.'

'Ah!' She shook her head. 'Very wrong —very wrong! Many have been robbed at Shadwell. But come in, and I will tell you some of my troubles. Do take a chair.'

She drew out a handkerchief, and wiped a rising tear.

'Dear me, what a delightful thing to see a young fellow like you—not drowned yet!'

'I might have been,' he replied, 'but for——'

'Ah, and you may be yet.' This seemed a very cheerful person. 'Many no older than yourself are lying at the bottom of the sea this minute.'

'That is very true,' he said, 'but——'

'Oh, I know what you would say. And Captain Zachariasen eighty-six years of age if a day.'

The young man began to feel as if he had got into an enchanted palace.

When Lal found him there, he was sitting bolt upright, while Mrs. Rydquist was discoursing at large on perils and disasters at sea.

'You yourself,' she was saying, 'look like one who will go early and find your end——'

'Gracious, mother!' cried Lal, in her quick, sharp way, 'how can you say such things? Time enough when he does go to find it out. Besides —— Your clothes are quite dry now, and—oh! oh! oh!'

Then she laughed again, seeing the delightful incongruity of trousers, sleeves, arms, and legs, so that he retired in confusion.

When he came to put on his own things, he discovered that the girl of the boat—this girl so remarkably handy with her sculls—had actually taken the opportunity to restore a button to the back of his neck. The loss of this button had troubled him for two voyages and a half. So delicate and unusual an attention naturally went straight to his heart, which was already softened by the consideration of the girl's bravery and beauty.

He thought she looked prettier than ever, with her large eyes and the sweet innocence of her face, when he came down again in his uniform.

'Your steward is dry, too,' she said, 'and warming himself before the kitchen fire. Will you have some tea with the Captains? It is their tea-time.'

'I would rather have some tea with **you**,' he replied, 'if I might.'

'Would you? Then of course you shall.'

She spoke as if it were a mere nothing, a trifle of no value at all, this invitation to take tea with her.

She took him into her own room, where the young man had seen the old fellow asleep, and presently brewed him a cup of tea, the like of which, he thought, he had never tasted, and set before him a plate of hot toast.

'That is better for you,' she said, as wisely as any doctor, 'than hot brandy and water.'

At last he rose, after drinking as much tea as

he could and staying as long as he dared. The ship would be in dock by this time. He must get across.

'May I come over, when I can get away, to see you again?' he asked, bashfully.

She replied, without any bashfulness at all and with straightforward friendliness, that she would be very glad to see him whenever he could call upon her, and that the best time would be in the afternoon, or, as the evenings were now long, in the evening; but not in the morning, when she was busy with all sorts of things, and especially in superintending the Captains' dinner.

'I will come,' he said, and this time he blushed. 'What is your name?'

'I am Lal Rydquist,' she replied, as if everybody ought to know her. But that was not at all what she meant.

'Lal! What a pretty name. It suits——' And here he stopped and blushed again.

'And what is your name?'

'Rex Armiger,' he said. 'And I am second officer on board the "Aryan," of the Indian Peninsular line, homeward bound from Calcutta.'

This was the beginning of Lal's love-story. A young fellow, gallant and handsome, pulled dripping out of the river—a sailor, too—how could Lal fall in love with anybody but a sailor?

Every love-story has its dawn, its first faint glimmering, which grows into a glorious rose of day. There are generally, as we know, clouds about the east at the dawn of day. Clubmen about Pall Mall frequently remark this in the month of June on leaving the whist-table; policemen have told me the same thing; milkmen, in spring and autumn, report the phenomenon; old-fashioned poets observed it. There can be no real doubt or question about it. After the dawn and the morning comes the noon, when the story becomes uninteresting to outsiders, yet is a very delightful story to the actors themselves. There are different kinds of clouds, and you already know pretty well what was the cloud which for a long time made poor Lal's story a sad one.

When, however, the first streaks of dawn appeared the sky was cloudless. You must not suppose that this young lady beheld the man and straightway fell in love with him. Not at all. Love is a plant which takes time to grow. In her case it kept on growing long after Rex had left her; long, indeed, after everybody said he was dead. But it cannot be denied that she thought about him.

The Captains congratulated her on having pulled the young fellow out of the river. Captain Zachariasen, with a gallantry beyond his years, even went so far as to wish he had himself been the subject of the immersion and the rescue.

He also related several stories of his own daring, fifty, sixty, or seventy years before, in various parts of the ocean. All this was pleasing.

Lal laughed at the compliments and sang the more about the house, nor did it disturb her in the least when her mother lifted up her voice in prophecy.

'My dear,' she said, 'mark my words. If ever I saw shipwreck and drowning—I mean quite young drowning—on any man's face, it is marked on the face of that young man. The heedless and the giddy may laugh; but we know better, my dear—we who have gone through it.'

When a ship comes home and has but three weeks in which to discharge her cargo and take in her new lading, the officers have by no means an easy time. It is not holiday with them, but quite the reverse; and it was not often that Rex could get even an evening free. In fact, the whole of his wooing was accomplished in five visits to Rotherhithe.

On his first visit he was disappointed. Lal was on the river in her boat, and so he sat with her mother and waited. Mrs. Rydquist took the opportunity, which might never occur again, of solemnly warning him against falling in love with her daughter. This, she said, was a very possible thing to happen, especially for a sailor, because her girl was well set-up, not to say handsome.

Therefore, it was her duty to warn him, as she had already warned a good many, including Captain Skantlebury, afterwards cast away in Torres Straits, that it was an unlucky thing to marry into a family whose husbands and male relations generally found a grave at the bottom of the sea. Further, it was well known among sailors that if you rescued a person from drowning, that person would, at some time or other, repay your offices by injuring your earthly prospects. So that there were two excellent reasons why Rex should avoid the Rock of Love.

They were doubtless valid; but they were not strong enough to repress in the young man a look of joy and admiration when the girl came home fresh and bright as an ocean nymph. He took supper with her, and between them the two managed to repress the gloom even of the prophetess who sat with them, as cheerful as Cassandra at a Trojan supper. Did ever anyone consider how much that good old man King Priam had to put up with?

Another time was on a Sunday evening. They went to church together and sang out of the same hymn-book. Captain Zachariasen was in the pew also, and he went to sleep three times— viz., during the first lesson, the second lesson, and the sermon, without counting the prayers, during which he probably dropped off as well. After the service, as the evening was fine and the air warm, they sat awhile in the churchyard, and the young fellow, seated on a tombstone, unconscious of the moral he was illustrating, had a very good time indeed talking with Lal. When they were tired of the churchyard they walked away to the bridge over the entrance to the docks, and leaned over the rail talking still. Lal was quite used to the confidences of her friends, but somehow this one's confidences were different. He sought no advice, he confessed no love-affair; he did not begin to look at her as if he was struck silly, and then ask her to marry him—which so many of the Captains had done; he asked her about herself, and seemed eager to know all she would tell him, as if there was anything about herself that so gallant a sailor would care to know, with such stupid particulars about her daily life, and how she never left Rotherhithe at all, and had seen no other place.

'What a strange life!' he said, after many questions. 'What a dull life! Are you not tired of it?'

'No,' she answered. 'Why should I be? Do they not bring a constant change into the house, my Captains? I know all their adventures, and I could tell you, oh! such stories. You should hear Captain Zachariasen when he begins to recollect.'

'Ay, ay, we can all spin yarns. But never to leave this place!' He paused, with a sigh.

'I am happy,' said Lal. 'Tell me about yourself.'

It was her turn now, and she began to question him until he told all he had to tell; but I suppose he kept back something, as one is told to leave something on the dish, for good manners. But if he did not tell all, it was because he was modest, not because he had things to hide of which he was ashamed.

He was, he said, the son of a Lincolnshire clergyman, and he was destined to the Church; solemnly set apart, he was, by his parents and consecrated in early infancy. This made his subsequent conduct the more disgraceful, although, as he pleaded, his own consent was not asked nor his inclinations consulted. The road to the Church is grievously beset by wearisome boulders, pits, ditches, briars, and it may be fallen trunks, which some get over without the least difficulty, whereas to others they are grievous hindrances. These things are an allegory, and I mean books. Now unlucky Rex, a masterly youth in all games, schoolboy feats, fights, freaks, and fanteegs, regarded a book, from his earliest infancy, unless it was a romance of the sea or story of adventure, with a dislike and suspicion amounting almost to mania. In his recital to Lal, he avoided mention of the many floggings he received, the battles he fought, and the insubordination of which he was guilty, and the countless lessons which he had not learned. He simply said that he ran away from school and got to Liverpool, where, after swopping clothes with a real sailor boy, he got on board a Canadian brig as loblolly boy, and was kicked and cuffed all the way to Quebec and all the way back again. The skipper cuffed him, the mate cuffed him, the cook cuffed him, the crew cuffed him; he got rough treatment and bad grub. His faculties were stimulated, no doubt, and a good foundation laid for smartness in after life as a sailor. Also, his frame was hardened by the fresh breeze of the Windy Fifties. On his return, he wrote to his father, to say that he was about to return to school. He did return; was the hero of the school for two months, and then again ran away and tried the sea once more, from Glasgow to New York in a cargo steamer. Finally, his father had to renounce his ambitious schemes, in spite of the early consecration and setting apart, and got him entered as a middy in the service of a great line of steamers. Now, at the age of twenty-two, he was second officer.

Such was the modesty of the young man that he omitted to state many remarkable facts in his own life, though these redounded greatly to his credit; nor was it till afterwards that Lal discovered how good a character he bore for steady seamanship and pluck, how well he stood for promotion. Also, he did not tell her that he was the softest-hearted fellow in the world, though his knuckles were so hard; that he was the easiest man in the world to lead, although the hardest to drive; that on board he was always ready, when off duty, to act as nursemaid, protector, and playfellow for any number of children; that he was also at such times as good as a son or a brother to all ladies on board; that on shore he was ever ready to give away all his money to the first who asked for it; that he thought no evil of his neighbour; that he considered all women as angels, but Lal as an archangel; and that he was modest, thinking himself a person of the very smallest importance on account of these difficulties over books, and a shameful apostate in the matter of the falling off from the early dedication.

When a young woman begins to take a real interest in the adventures of a young man, and, like Desdemona, to ask questions, she generally lays a solid foundation for much more than mere interest. Dido, though she was no longer in her *première jeunesse*, is a case in point, as well as Desdemona. And every married person recollects the flattering interest taken in each other by *fiancé* and *fiancée* during the early days, the sweet sun-shiny days, of their engagement.

That Sunday night, after the talk in the church-yard, they went back to the house, and Rex had supper with the Captains, winning golden opinions by his great and well-sustained powers over cold beef and pickles. After this they smoked pipes and told yarns, and Lal sat among them by the side of Rex, which was a joy to him, though she was sitting on the arm of Captain Zachariasen's wooden chair, and not his own.

On another occasion during that happy and never-to-be-forgotten three weeks, Rex carried the girl across the river and showed her his own ship lying in the East India Docks, which, she was fain to confess, are finer than the Commercial Docks. He took her all over the great and splendid vessel, showed her the saloon with its velvet couches, hanging lamps, gilt ornaments, and long tables in the officers' quarters; and midships, and the sailors' for'ard; took her down to the engine-room by a steep ladder of polished iron bars, showed her the bridge, the steering tackle, and the captain's cabin, in which he lowered his voice from reverence as one does in a church. When she had seen everything, he invited her to return to the saloon, where she found a noble repast spread, and the chief officer, the third mate, the Purser, and the Doctor waiting to be introduced to her.   They paid her so much attention and deference; they said so many kind things about her courage and presence of mind; they waited on her so jealously; they were so kind to her, that the girl was ashamed.   She was so very ignorant, you see, of the power of beauty.   Then a bottle of champagne, a drink which Lal had heard of but never seen, was produced, and they all drank to her health, bowing and smiling, first to her and then to Rex, who blushed and hung his head.   Then it appeared that every man had something which he ardently desired her to accept, and when Lal came away Rex had his arms full of pretty Indian things, smelling of sandal-wood, presents to her from his brother-officers.   This, she thought, was very kind of them, especially as they had never seen her before.   And then Dick, the officers' steward, the deaf and dumb Malay whom she had helped to pull out of the water, came and kissed her hand humbly, in token of gratitude.   A beautiful and wonderful day.   Yet what did the Doctor mean when they came away? For while the Purser stood at one end of the gangway, and the chief officer at the other, and the third mate in the middle, all to see her safe across, the Doctor, left behind on board, slapped Rex loudly upon the shoulder and laughed, saying :—

'Gad! Rex, you're a lucky fellow!'

How was he lucky? she asked him in the boat, and said she should be glad to hear of good luck for him. But he only blushed and made no reply.

One of the things which she brought home after this visit was a certain grey parrot. He had no particular value as a parrot. There were many more valuable parrots already about the house, alive or stuffed. But this bird had accomplishments, and among other things, he knew his master's name, and would cry, to everybody's admiration : 'Poor Rex Armiger! Poor Rex Armiger!'

When Lal graciously accepted this gift, the young man took it as a favourable sign. She had already, he knew, sent away a dozen Captains at least, and he was only second mate. Yet still, when a girl takes such a present she means—she surely means to make some difference.

Then there was one day more—the last day but one before the ship sailed—the last opportunity that Rex could find before they sailed. He had leave. for a whole day ; the lading was completed, the passengers were sending on their boxes and trunks ; the Purser and the stewards were taking in provisions—mountains of provisions, with bleating sheep, milch cows, cocks and hens —for the voyage.

All was bustle and stir at the Docks, but there

was no work for the second officer.   He presented himself at Seven Houses at ten o'clock in the morning, without any previous notice, and proposed, if you please, nothing short of a whole day out.   A whole day, mind you, from that moment until ten o'clock at night.   Never was proposal more revolutionary.

'All day long?' she cried, her great eyes full of surprise and joy.

'All day,' he said, 'if you will trust yourself with me.   Where shall we go?'

'Where?' she repeated.

I suppose that now and then some echoes reach Rotherhithe of the outer world and its amusements.   Presumably there are natives who have seen the Crystal Palace and other places; here and there might be found one or two who have seen a theatre.   Most of them, however, know nothing of any place of amusement whatever.   It is a city without any shows.   Punch and Judy go not near it; Cheap Jack passes it by; the wandering feet of circus horses never pass that way; gipsies' tents have never been seen there; the boys of Rotherhithe do not know even the travelling caravan with the fire-eater.   To conjurers, men with entertainments, and lecturers it is an untrodden field. When Lal came, in a paper, upon the account of festive doings she passed them over, and turned to the condition of the markets in South Africa or

Quebec as being a subject more likely to interest the Captains. Out of England there were plenty of things to interest her. She knew something about the whole round world, or, at least, its harbours ; but of London she was ignorant.

'Where?' she asked, gasping.

'There's the Crystal Palace and Epping Forest ; there's the National Gallery and Highgate Hill; there's the top of St. Paul's and the Aquarium ; there's Kew Gardens and the Tower ; there's South Kensington and Windsor Castle '— Rex bracketed the places according to some obscure arrangement in his own mind—'lots of places. The only thing is where?'

'I have seen none of them,'she replied. 'Will you choose for me?'

'Oh!' he groaned. 'Here is a house full of great hulking skippers, and she works herself to death for them, and not one among them all has ever had the grace to take her to go and see something!'

'Don't call them names,' she replied, gently ; ' our people never go anywhere, except to Poplar and Limehouse. One of them went one evening to Woolwich Gardens, but he did not like it. He said the manners of the people were forward, and he was cheated out of half a crown.'

'Then, Lal,' he jumped up and made a great show of preparing for immediate departure with his cap; 'then, Lal, let us waste no more time in talking, but be off at once.'

'Oh, I can't!'

Her face fell, and the tears came into her eyes as she suddenly recollected a reason why she could not go.

'Why can't you?'

'Because—oh, because of the pudding. I can trust her with the potatoes, and she will boil the greens to a turn. But the pudding I always make, and no one else can make it but me.'

The lady referred to was not her mother, but the assistant—the 'service.'

'Can't they go without pudding for once?'

Lal shook her head.

'They always expect pudding, and they are very particular about the currants. You can't think what a quantity of currants they want in their pudding.'

'Do you always give them plum-duff, then?'

'Except when they have roly-poly or apple dumplings. Sometimes it is baked plum-duff, sometimes it is boiled, sometimes with sauce, and sometimes with brandy. But I think they would never forgive me if there was no pudding.'

Rex nodded his head, put on his cap—this conversation took place in the kitchen—and marched resolutely straight into the Captains' room, where three of them were at that moment sitting in conversation. One was Captain Zachariasen.

'Gentlemen,' he said, politely saluting; 'Lal wants a whole holiday. But she says she can't take it unless you will kindly go without your pudding to-day.'

They looked at each other. No one for a time spoke. The gravity of the proposal was such that no one liked to take the responsibility of accepting it. A dinner at Rydquist's without pudding was a thing hitherto unheard of.

'Why,' asked Captain Zachariasen, severely—'why, if you please, Mr. Armiger, does Lal want a holiday to-day? And why cannot she be content with a half-holiday? Do I ever take a whole day?'

'Because she wants to go somewhere with me,' replied Rex, stoutly; 'and if she doesn't go to-day she won't go at all, because we sail the day after to-morrow.'

'Under these circumstances, gentlemen,' said Captain Zachariasen, softening, and feeling that he had said enough for the assertion of private rights, 'seeing that Lal is, for the most part, an obliging girl, and does her duty with a willing spirit, I think—you are agreed with me, gentlemen?'

The other two nodded their heads, but with some sadness.

'Then, sir,' said Captain Zachariasen, as if he

were addressing his chief officer at high noon,
' make it so.'

' Now,' said Rex, as they passed Rotherhithe
parish church and drew near unto Thames Tunnel
Station, ' I've made up my mind where to take
you to. As for the British Museum, it's sticks
and stones, and South Kensington is painted pots;
the National Gallery is saints and sign-boards;
the Crystal Palace is buns, and boards, and ginger-
beer, with an organ; the Monument of London is
no better than the crosstrees. Where we will go,
Lal—where we will go for our day out—is to
Hampton Court, and we will have such a day as
you shall remember.'

There had been, as yet, no word of love; but
he called her Lal, and she called him Rex, which
is an excellent beginning.

They did have that day; they did go to
Hampton Court. First they drove in a hansom—
Lal thought nothing could be more delightful than
this method of conveyance—to Waterloo Station,
where they were so lucky as to catch a train
going to start in three-quarters of an hour, and
by that they went to Hampton Court.

It was .in the early days of the month of
June, which in England has two moods. One is
the dejected, make-yourself-as-miserable-as-you-
can mood, when the rain falls dripping all the

day, and the leaves, which have hardly yet fully formed on the trees, begin to get rotten before their time, and think of falling off. That mood of June is not delightful. The other, which is far preferable, is that in which the month comes with a gracious smile, bearing in her hands lilac, roses, laburnum, her face all glorious with sunshine, soft airs, and warmth. Then the young year springs swiftly into vigorous manhood, with fragrance and sweet perfumes, and the country hedges are splendid with their wealth of a thousand wild flowers, and the birds sing above their nests. Men grow young men again, lapped and wrapped in early summer; the blood of the oldest is warmed; their fancies run riot; they begin to babble of holidays, to talk of walks in country places, of rest on hill-sides, of wanderings, rod in hand, beside the streams, of shady woods, and the wavelets of a tranquil sea; they feel once more —one must feel it every year again or die—the old simple love for earth, fair mother-earth, generous earth, mother, nurse, and fosterer—as well as grave; they enjoy the sunshine. Sad autumn is as yet far off, and seems much farther; they are not yet near unto the days when they shall say, one to the other:

'Lo! the evil days are come when we may say, "I have no pleasure in them."'

The train sped forth from the crowded houses,

and presently passed into the fields and woods of Surrey. Rex and Lal were alone in a second-class carriage, and she looked out of the window while he looked at her. And so to Hampton, where the Mole joins the silver Thames, and the palace stands beside the river bank.

I have always thought that to possess Hampton Court is a rare and precious privilege which Londoners cannot regard with sufficient gratitude, for, with the exception of Fontainebleau, which is too big, there is nothing like it—except, perhaps, in Holland—anywhere. It is delightful to wander in the cool cloisters, about the bare chambers hung with pictures, and in the great empty hall, where the Queen might dine every day if she chose, her crown upon her head, with braying of trumpets, scraping of fiddles, and pomp of scarlet retainers. But she does not please. Then one may walk over elastic turf, round beds of flowers, or down long avenues of shady trees, which make one think of William the Third; or one may look over a wooden garden gate into what was the garden in the times before Cardinal Wolsey found out this old country grange and made it into a palace. Young people—especially young people in love—may also seek the windings of the maze.

This boy Rex, with the girl who seemed to him the most delightful creature ever formed by a benevolent Providence, enjoyed all these delights, the girl lost in what seemed to her a dream of wonder. Why had she never seen any of these beautiful places? For the first time in her life, Rotherhithe, and the docks and ships, became small to her. She had never before known the splendour of stately halls, pictures, or great gardens. She felt humiliated by her strangeness, and to this day, though now she has seen a great many splendid places, she regards Hampton Court as the most wonderful and the most romantic of all buildings ever erected, and I do not think she is far wrong.

One thing only puzzled her. She had read, somewhere, of the elevating influences of art. This is a great gallery of art. Yet somehow she did not feel elevated at all. Especially did a collection of portraits of women—all with drooping eyes and false smiles and strange looks, the meaning of which she knew not—make her long to hurry out of the room and into the fair gardens, on whose lawns she could forget these pictures. How could they elevate or improve the people? Art, you see, only elevates those who understand a little of the technique, and ordinary people go to the picture-galleries for the story told by each picture. This is the reason why the contemplation of a vast number of pictures has hitherto failed to improve our culture or to elevate our standards. But these two, like most visitors, took all for granted, and it must be owned that there are many excellent stories, especially those of the old sea-fight pictures, in the Hampton Court galleries.

Then they had dinner together in a room whose windows looked right down the long avenue of Bushey, where the chestnuts were in all their glory; and after dinner Rex took her on the river. It was the same river as that of Rotherhithe. But who would have thought that twenty miles would make so great a change? No ships, no steamers, no docks, no noise, no shouting, no hammering. And what a difference in the boats! They drifted slowly down with the silent current. The warm sun of the summer afternoon lay lovingly on the meadows. It was not a Saturday. No one was on the river but themselves. The very swans sat sleepily on the water; there was a gentle swish and slow murmur of the current along the reeds and grasses of the bank; crimson and golden leaves hung over the river; the flowers of the lilies were lying open on the water.

Lal held the ropes and Rex the sculls; but he let them lie idle and looked at the fair face before him, while she gazed dreamily about, thinking how she should remember, and by what things, this wonderful day, this beautiful river, this palace, and this gentle rowing in the light skiff. As she looked, the smile faded out of her face and her eyes filled with tears.

'Why, Lal?' he asked.

She made no reply for a minute or two, thinking what reason she might truthfully allege for her tears, which had risen unbidden at the touch of some secret chord.

'I do not know,' she said. 'Except that everything is so new and strange, and I am quite happy, and it is all so beautiful.'

Rex reflected on the superior nature of women who can shed tears as a sign of happiness.

'I am so happy,' he said, 'that I should like to dance and sing, except that I am afraid of capsizing the craft, when to Davy's locker we should go for want of your dingy, Lal.'

But they could not stay on the river all the evening. The sun began to descend; clouds came up from the south-west; the wind freshened; a mist arose, and the river became sad and mysterious.

Then Rex turned the bows and rowed back.

The girl shuddered as she stepped upon the shore.

'I shall never forget it,' she said; 'never. And now it is all over.'

'Will you remember, with this day, your companion of the day?' asked Rex.

'Yes,' she replied, with the frank and truthful

gaze which went straight to the young man's heart; 'I shall never forget the day or my companion.'

They went back to the palace, and while the shadows grew deeper, walked in the old-fashioned garden of King William, beneath its arch of branches, old now and knotty and gnarled.

Rex was to sail in two days' time. He would have no other chance. Yet he feared to break the charm.

'We must go,' he said. 'Yes, it is all over.' He heaved a mighty sigh. 'What a day we have had. And now it is gone, it is growing dark, and we must go. And this is the last time I shall see you, Lal.'

'Yes,' she murmured, 'the last time.'

Years afterwards she remembered those words and the thought of ill omens and what they may mean.

'The last time,' she repeated.

'I suppose you know, Lal, that I love you?' said Rex, quite simply. 'You must know that. But, of course, everybody loves you.'

'Oh!' she laid her hand upon his arm. 'Are you sure, quite sure, that you love me? You might be mistaken, Rex.'

'Sure, Lal?'

'Can you really love me?'

'My darling, have not other men told you

the same thing?   Have you not listened and sent them away?   Do not send me away, too, Lal.'

'They said they—— Oh, it was nonsense. They could not really have loved me, because I did not love them at all.'

'And—and—me?' asked Rex, with fine disregard of grammar.

'Oh, no, Rex.   I do not want to send you away—not if you really love me;——and, Rex, Rex, you have kissed me enough.'

They could not go away quite then; they stayed there till they were found by the custodian of the vine, who ignominiously led them to the palace-gates and dismissed them with severity. Then Rex must needs have supper, in order to keep his sweetheart with him a little longer. And it was not till the ten o'clock train that they returned to town: Lal quiet and a little tearful, her hand in her lover's; Rex full of hope and faith and charity, and as happy as if he were, indeed, 'rex orbis totius,' the king of the whole world.

At half-past eleven he brought her home   It was very late for Rotherhithe; the Captains were mostly in bed by ten, and all the lights out, but to-night Mrs. Rydquist sat waiting for her daughter.

'Mrs. Rydquist,' said the young man, beaming like a sun-god between the pair of candles over which the good lady sat reading, 'she has promised to be my wife—Lal is going to marry me. The day after to-morrow we drop down the river, but I shall be home again soon—home again. Come Lal, my darling, my sweet, my queen,' he took her in his arms and kissed her again—this shameless young sailor—'and as soon as I get my ship — why — why — why——' he kissed her once more, and yet once more.

'I wish you, young man,' said Lal's mother, in funereal tones, ' a better fate than has befallen all the men who fell in love with us. I have already given you my most solemn warning. You rush upon your fate, but I wash my hands of it. My mother's lost husband, and my husband, lie dead at the bottom of the sea. Also two of my first cousins' husbands, and a second cousin's once-removed husband. We are an unlucky family; but, perhaps, my daughter's husband may be more fortunate.'

'Oh, mother,' cried poor Lal, ' don't make us down-hearted !'

'I said, my dear,' she replied, folding her hands with a kind of resignation to the inevitable, 'I said that I hope he may be more fortunate. I cannot say more ; if I could say more I would say it. If I think he may not be more fortunate, I will not say it ; nor will I give you pain, Mr.

Armiger, by prophesying that you will add to
our list.'

'Never mind,' said Rex; 'we sailors are
mostly as safe at sea as the landlubbers on shore,
only people won't think so. Heart up, Lal!
Heart up, my sweet! Come outside and say
good-bye.'

'Look!' said Mrs. Rydquist, pointing cheerfully to the candlestick, when her daughter returned with tears in her eyes and Rex's last kiss
burning on her lips; 'there is a winding-sheet, my
dear, in the candle. To-night a coffin popped
out of the kitchen-fire. I took it up in hopes it
might have been a purse. No, my dear, a coffin.
Captain Zachariasen crossed knives at dinner to-
day. I have had shudders all the evening, which
is as sure a sign of graves as any I know. Before
you came home the furniture cracked three times.
No doubt, my dear, these warnings are for me,
who am a poor, weak creature, and ready and
willing and hopeful, I am sure, to be called
away; or for Captain Zachariasen, who is, to be
sure, a great age, and should expect his call
every day instead of going on with his talk and
his rum and his pipe as if he was forgotten; or
for any one of the Captains, afloat or ashore;
these signs, my dear, may be meant for anybody,
and I would not be so presumptuous in a house
full of sailors as to name the man for whom they

have come; but, if I read signs right, then they mean that young man.   And oh! my poor girl——' she clasped her hands as if now, indeed, there could be no hope.

'What is it, mother?'

'My dear, it is a Friday, of all the days in the week!'

She rose, took a candle, and went to bed, with her handkerchief to her eyes.

CHAPTER IV.

OVERDUE AND POSTED.

THIS day of days, this queen of all days, too swiftly sped over the first and last of the young sailor's wooing. Lal's sweetheart was lost to her almost as soon as he was found. But he left her so happy in spite of her mother's gloomy forebodings, that she wondered—not knowing that all the past years had been nothing but a long preparation for the time of love—how could she ever have been happy before? And she was only eighteen, and her lover as handsome as Apollo, and as well-mannered. Next morning at about twelve o'clock she jumped into her boat and rowed out upon the river to see the 'Aryan' start upon her voyage. The tide was on the turn and the river full when the great steamer came out of dock and slowly made her way upon the crowded water a miracle of human skill, a great and wonderful living thing, which, though even a clumsy lighter might sink and destroy it, yet could live through the wildest storm ever known in the Sea of Cyclones, through which she was to sail. As the 'Aryan' passed the little boat Lal saw her lover. He had sprung upon the bulwark and was waving his hat in farewell. Oh, gallant Rex, so brave and so loving! To think that this glorious creature, this god-like man, this young prince among sailors, should fall in love with her! And then the doctor, and the purser, and the chief officers, and even the captain, came to the side and took off their caps to her, and some of the passengers, informed by the doctor who she was, and how brave she was, waved their hands and cheered.

Then the ship forged ahead, and in a few minutes Rex jumped down with a final kiss of his fingers. The screw turned more quickly; the ship forged ahead. Lal lay to in mid-stream, careless what might run into her, gazing after her with straining eyes. When she had rounded the point and was lost to view, the girl, for the first time in her life since she was a child, burst into tears and sobbing.

It was but a shower. Lal belonged to a sailor family. Was she to weep and go in sadness because her lover was away doing his duty upon the blue water? Not so. She shook her head, dried her eyes, and rowed homewards, grave yet cheerful.

'Is his ship gone?' asked her mother.

'Well, he is a fine lad to look at, Lal, and if he is as true as he is strong and well-favoured, I could wish you nothing better. Let us forget the signs and warnings, my dear'—this was kindly meant, but had an unpleasant and gruesome sound—'and let us hope that he will come back again. Indeed, I do not see any reason why he should not come back more than once.'

Everything went on, then, as if nothing had happened. What a strange thing it is that people can go on as if nothing had happened, after the most tremendous events! Life so changed for her, yet Captain Zachariasen taking up the thread of her discourse just as before, and the same interest expected to be shown in the timber trade! Yet what a very different thing is interest in timber trade compared with interest in a man! Then she discovered with some surprise that her old admiration of captains as a class had been a good deal modified during the last three weeks. There were persons in the world, it was now quite certain, of culture superior even to that of a skipper in the Canadian trade. And she clearly discovered, for the first time, that a whole life devoted to making captains comfortable, providing them with pudding, looking after their linen, and hearing their confidences, might, without the gracious influences of love, become a very arid and barren kind of life. Perhaps, also, the recollection of that holiday at Hampton Court helped to modify her views on the subject of Rotherhithe and its people. The place was only, after all, a small part of a great city; the people were humble. One may discover as much certainly about one's own people without becoming ashamed of them. It is only when one reaches a grade higher in the social scale that folk become ashamed of themselves. An assured position in the world, as the chimney-sweep remarked, gives one confidence. Lal plainly saw that her sweetheart was of gentler birth and better breeding than she had been accustomed to. She therefore resolved to do her best never to make him on that-account repent his choice, and there was an abundance of fine sympathy—the assumption or pretence of which is the foundation of good manners—in this girl's character.

It was an intelligent parrot which Rex had given her, and at this juncture proved a remarkably sympathetic creature, for at the sight of his mistress he would shake his head, plume his wings, and presently, as if necessary to console her, would cry :

'Poor Rex Armiger ! Poor Rex Armiger !'

But she was never dull, nor did she betray to anyone, least of all to her old friend Captain Zachariasen, that her manner of regarding things had in the least degree changed, while the secret joy that was in her heart showed itself in a thousand merry ways, with songs and laughter, and little jokes with her captains, so that they marvelled that the existence of a sweetheart at sea should produce so beneficial an effect upon maidens. Perhaps, too, in some mysterious way, her happiness affected the puddings. I say not this at random, because certainly the fame of Rydquist's as a house where comforts, elsewhere unknown, and at Limehouse and Poplar quite unsuspected, could be found, spread far and wide, even to Deptford on the east, and Stepney on the north, and the house might have been full over and over again, but they would take in no strangers, being in this respect as exclusive as Boodle's.

This attitude of cheerfulness was greatly commended by Captain Zachariasen. 'Some girls,' he said, ' would have let their thoughts run upon their lover instead of their duty, whereby houses are brought to ruin and captains seek comfort elsewhere. Once the sweetheart is gone, he ought never more to be thought upon till he comes home again, save in bed or in church, while there is an egg to be boiled or an onion to be peeled.'

The first letter which Rex sent her was the first that Lal had ever received in all her life. And such a letter ! It came from the Suez Canal; the next came from Aden ; the next from Point de Galle ; the next from Calcutta. So far all was well. Be sure that Lal read them over and over again, every one, and carried them about in her bosom, and knew them all word for word, and was, after the way of a good and honest girl, touched to the very heart that a man should love her so very, very much, and should think so highly of her, and should talk as if she was all goodness—a thing which no woman can understand. It makes silly girls despise men, and good girls respect and fear them.

The next letter was much more important than the first four, which were, in truth, mere rhapsodies of passion, although on that very account more interesting than letters which combine matter-of-fact business with love, for, on arriving at Calcutta, Rex found a proposal waiting for his acceptance. This offer came from the Directors of the Company, and showed in what good esteem he was held, being nothing less than the command of one of their smaller steamers, engaged in what is called the country trade.

'It will separate us for three years at least,' he wrote, 'and perhaps for five, but I cannot afford to refuse the chance. Perhaps, if I did, I might never get another offer, and everybody is congratulating me, and thinking me extremely fortunate to get a ship so early. So, though it keeps me from the girl of my heart, I have accepted, and I sail at once. My ship is named the " Philippine." She is a thousand-ton boat, and classed 100 A1, newly built. She is not like the " Aryan," fitted with splendid mirrors and gold and paint and a great saloon, being built chiefly for cargo. The crew are all Lascars, and I am the only Englishman aboard except the mate and the chief engineer. We are under orders to take in rice from Hong-Kong; bound for Brisbane, first of all; if that answers we shall continue in the country grain trade; if not, we shall, I suppose, go seeking, when I shall have a commission on the cargo. As for pay, I am to have twenty pounds a month, with rations and allowances, and liberty to trade—so many tons every voyage—if I like. These are good terms, and at the end of every year there should be something put by in the locker. Poor Lal! Oh, my dear sweet eyes! Oh, my dear brown hair! Oh, my dear sweet lips! I shall not kiss them for three years more. What are three years? Soon gone, my pretty. Think of that, and heart up! As soon as I can I will try for a Port-of-London ship. Then we will be married and have a house at Gravesend, where you shall see me come up stream, homeward bound.' With much more to the same effect.

Three years—or it might be five! Lal put down the letter, and tried to make out what it would mean to her. She would be in three years, when Rex came home, one and twenty, and he would be five and twenty. Five and twenty seems 'to eighteen what forty seems to thirty, fifty to forty, and sixty to fifty. One has a feeling that the ascent of life must then be quite accomplished, and the descent fairly begun ; the leaves on the trees by the wayside must be ever so little browned and dusty, if not yellow ; the heart must be full of experience, the head must be full of wisdom, the crown of glory, if any is to be worn at all, already on the brows. The ascent of life is like the climbing of some steep hill, because the summit seems continually to recede, and so long as one is young in heart it is never reached. Rex five and twenty! Three years to wait!

It is, indeed, a long time for the young to look forward to. Such a quantity of things get accomplished in three years! Why, in three years a lad gets through his whole undergraduate course, and makes a spoon or spoils a horn. Three years makes up one hundred and fifty-six weeks, with the same number of Sundays, in every one of which a girl may sit in the quiet church and wonder on what wild seas or in what peaceful haven her lover may be floating. Three years are four summers in the course of three years, with as many other seasons ; in three years there is time for many a hope to spring up, flourish for a while, and die ; for friendship to turn into hate; for strength to decay; and for youth to grow old. The experience of the long succession of human generations has developed this sad thing among mankind that we cannot look forward with joy to the coming years, and in everything unknown which will happen to us we expect a thing of evil. Three years! Yet it must be borne, as the lady said to the school-boy concerning the fat beef, 'It is helped, and must be finished.'

When Mrs. Rydquist heard the news she first held up her hands, and spread them slowly outwards, shaking and wagging her head—a most dreadful sign, worse than any of those with which Panurge discomfited Thaumast. Then she sighed heavily. Then she said aloud: 'Oh! dear, dear, dear! So soon! I had begun to hope that the bad luck would not show yet! Dear, dear! Yet what could be expected after such certain signs?'

'Why,' said Captain Zachariasen, 'as for signs, they may mean anything or anybody, and as for fixing them on Cap'en Armiger, no reason that I can see. Don't be downed, Lal. The narrow seas are as safe as the Mediterranean. In my time there were the pirates, who are now shot, hanged, and drowned, every man Jack. No more stinkpots in crawling boats pretending to be friendly traders. You might row your dingy about the islands as safe as Lime'us Reach. Lord! I'd rather go cruising with your sweetheart in them waters than take a twopenny omnibus along the Old Kent Road. Your signs, ma'am,' he said to Mrs. Rydquist, politely, 'must be read other ways. There's Cap'en Biddiman; perhaps they're meant for him.'

Then came another letter from Singapore. Rex was pleased with the ship and his crew. All was going well.

After six weeks there came another letter. It was from Hong-Kong. The 'Philippine' had taken on board her cargo of rice and was to sail next day.

Rex wrote in his usual confident, happy vein —full of love, of hope, and happiness.

After that—no more letters at all. Silence.

Lal went on in cheerfulness for a long time. Rex could not write from Brisbane. He would write when the ship got back to Hong-Kong.

The weeks went on, but still there was silence. It was whispered in the Captains' room that the 'Philippine' was long overdue at Moreton Bay. Then the whispers became questions whether there was any news of her: then one went across to the office of the company, and brought back the dreadful news that the owners had given her up; and they began to hide away the 'Shipping and Mercantile Gazette.' Then everybody became extremely kind to Lal, studying little surprises for her, and assuming an appearance of light-heartedness so as to deceive the poor girl. She went about with cheerful face, albeit with sinking heart. Ships are often overdue; letters get lost on the way. For a while she still carolled and sang about her work, though at times her song would suddenly stop like the song of a bullfinch, who remembers something, and must needs stay his singing while he thinks about it.

Then there came a time when the poor child stopped singing altogether, and would look with anxious eyes from one captain to the other, seeking comfort. But no one had any comfort to give her.

Captain Zachariasen told her at last. He was an old man; he had seen so many shipwrecks that they thought he would tell her best; also it was considered his duty, as the father or the oldest inhabitant of Rydquist's, to undertake this task; and as a wise and discreet person he would tell the story, as it should be told, in few words, and so get it over without beatings on and off. He accepted the duty, and discharged himself of it as soon as he could. He told her the story, in fact, the next morning in the kitchen.

He said, quietly:

'Lal, my dear, the " Philippine " has gone to the bottom, and—and don't take on, my pretty.

But Cap'en Armiger he is gone, too; with all hands he went down.'

'How do you know?' she asked. The news was sudden, but she felt it coming; that is, she had felt some of it—not all.

'The insurances have been all paid up; the ship is posted at Lloyd's. My dear, I went to the underwriter's a month ago and more, and axed about her. Axed what they would under-write her for, and they said a hundred per cent.; and then they wouldn't do it. Not an atom of hope—gone she is, and that young fellow aboard her. Well, my dear, that's done with. Shall I leave you here alone to get through a spell o' crying?'

'The ship,' said Lal, with dry eyes, 'may be at the bottom of the sea, and the insurances may be paid for her. But Rex is not drowned.'

That was what she said: 'Rex is not drowned.'

Her mother brought out her cherished crape —she was a woman whom this nasty, crinkling, black stuff comforted in a way—and offered to divide it with her daughter.

Lal refused; she bought herself gay ribbons and she decked herself with them. She tried, in order to show the strength of her faith, to sing about the house.

'Rex,' she said, stoutly, 'is not drowned.'

This was the most unexpected way of receiving the news. The captains looked for a burst of tears and lamentation, after which things would brighten up, and some other fellow might have a chance. No tears at all! No chance for anybody else!

'Ribbons!' moaned Mrs. Rydquist. 'Oh, Captain Zachariasen, my daughter wears ribbons—blue ribbons and red ribbons—while her sweetheart, lying at the bottom of the sea, cries aloud, poor lad, for a single yard of crape!'

''Twould be more natural,' said Captain Zachariasen, ' to cry and adone with it. But gals, ma'am, are not what gals was in my young days, when so many were there as was taken off by wars, privateers, storms, and the hand of the Lord, that there was no time to cry over them, not for more than a month or so. And as for flying in the face of Providence, and saying that a drowned man is not drowned—a man whose ship's insurances have been paid, and his ship actually posted at Lloyd's—why it's beyond anything.'

'Rex is not dead,' said the girl, to herself, again and again. ' He is not dead. I should know if he were dead. He would, somehow or other, come and tell me. He is sitting somewhere—I know not where it is—waiting for deliverance, and thinking—oh, my Rex! my Rex!—thinking about the girl he loves.'

This was what she said.   Her words were
brave, yet it is hard to keep one's faith up to so high
a level as these words demanded.   For no one else
thought there was, or could be, any chance.   For
nearly three years she struggled to keep alive this
poor ray of hope, based upon nothing at all ; and
for all that time no news came from the far East
about her lover's ship, nor did anyone know
where she was cast away or how.

Sometimes this faith would break down, and
she would ask in tears and with sobbings what so
many women bereft of their lovers have asked in
vain—an answer to her prayers.   Ah ! helpless
ones, if her prayers were mockeries and her lover
were dead in very truth !

CHAPTER V.

THE PATIENCE OF PENELOPE.

THE longer Ulysses stayed away from the rocky Ithaca the more numerous became the suitors for the hand of the lovely Penelope, who possessed the art, revived much later by Ninon de l'Enclos, of remaining beautiful although she grew old. That was because Penelope wickedly encouraged her lovers—to their destruction—and held out false hopes connected with a simple bit of embroidery. Why the foolish fellows, whose wits should have been sharpened by the vehemence of their passion, did not discover the trick, is not apparent. Perhaps, however, the climate of Ithaca was bracing and the wine good, so that they winked one upon the other, and pretended not to see, or whispered : 'He will never come, let us wait.'

The contrary proved the case with the lass of Rotherhithe. When, after two years or so, some of her old suitors ventured with as much delicacy as in them lay to reopen the subject of courtship, they were met with a reception so unmistakable, that they immediately retired, baffled, and in confusion ; some among them—those of coarser mind—to scoff and sneer at a constancy so unusual. Others—those of greater sympathies—to reflect with all humility on the great superiority of the feminine nature over their own, since it permitted a fidelity which they could not contemplate as possible for themselves, and were fain to admire, while they regretted it.

Gradually it became evident to most of them that the case was hopeless, and those captains who had once looked confidently to make Lal their own, returned to their former habits of friendly communications, and asked her advice and opinion in the matter of honourable proposals for the hands of other young ladies.

Three suitors still remained, and, each in his own way, refused to be sent away.

The first of these was Captain Holstius, whose acquaintance we have already made. He was, of course, in the Norway trade.

Perhaps it is not altogether fair to call Captain Holstius a suitor. He was a lover, but he had ceased to hope for anything except permission to go on in a friendly way, doing such offices as lay in his power, to please and help the girl whom he regarded—being a simple sort of fellow of a religious turn—as Dante regarded Beatrice. She was to him a mere angel of beauty and goodness ; in happier times she had been that rare and wonderful creature, a merry, laughing, happy angel, always occupied in good works, such as making plum-duff for poor humanity ; now, unhappily, an angel who endured suspense and the agony of long waiting for news which would never come.

For the good Norwegian, like all the rest, believed that Rex was dead long ago. Captain Holstius was not a man accustomed to put his thoughts into words ; nor did he, like a good many people, feel for thoughts through a multitude of phrases and thousands of words. But had he been able to set forth in plain language the things he intended and meant, he would certainly have said something to this effect. I think he would have said it more simply, and therefore with the greater force.

'If I could make her forget him : if I could substitute my own image entirely for the image of that dead man, so that she should be happy, just as she used to be when I first saw her, and if all could be as if he had never known her. I should think myself in heaven itself; or, if by taking another man to husband, and not me at all, she would recover her happiness, I should be contented, for I love her so much that all I ask is for her to be happy.'

It is a form of disinterested love which is so rare that at this moment I cannot remember any other single instance of it. Most people, when they love a girl, vehemently desire to keep her for themselves. Yet in the case of Captain Holstius, as for marrying her, that seemed a thing so remote from the region of probability, that he never now, whatever he had done formerly, allowed his thoughts to rest upon it, and contented himself with thinking what he could do for the girl; how he could soften the bitterness of her misfortune; how he could in small ways relieve the burden of her life, and make her a little happier.

Lal accepted all he gave, all his devotion and care. Little by little, because she saw Captain Holstius often, it became a pleasure to her to have him in the house. He became a sort of brother to her, who had never had that often unsatisfactory relative a brother, or, at all events, a true and unselfish friend, much better than the majority of brothers, who gave her everything and asked nothing for himself. She liked to be with him. They walked together about the wharves of the Commercial Docks in the quiet evenings; they rowed out together on the river in the little dingy, she sitting in the stern gazing upon the waters in silent thought, while the Norwegian dipped the sculls gently, looking with an ever-increasing sorrow in the face which had once been so full of sunshine, and now grew daily more overcast with cloud. They spoke little at such times to each other, or at any time ; but it seemed to her that she thought best, most hopefully, about Rex when she was with Captain Holstius. He was always a silent man, thinking that when he had a thing to say there would be no difficulty in saying it, and that if anyone had a thing to say unto him they could say it without any stimulus of talk from himself. Further, in the case of this poor Lal, what earthly good would it do to interrupt the girl in her meditations over a dead lover, by his idle chatter?

When they got home again she would thank him gently and return to her household duties, refreshed in spirit by this companionship in silence.

It is a maxim not sufficiently understood that the most refreshing thing in the world, when one is tired and sorry, disappointed or vexed, is to sit, walk, or remain for awhile silent with a silent friend whom you can trust not to chatter, or ask questions, or tease with idle observations. Pythagoras taught the same great truth, but obscurely and by an allegory. He enjoined silence among all his disciples for a term of years. This meant a companionship of silence, so as to forget the old friction and worry of the world.

The Norway ships come and go at quickly-recurring periods. Therefore Captain Holstius was much at the Commercial Docks, and had greater chances, if he had been the man to take advantage of them, than any of the other men. He was also favoured with the good opinion and the advocacy of Captain Zachariasen, who lost no opportunity of recommending Lal to consider her ways and at the same time the ways of the Norwegee. His admonition, we have seen, produced no effect. Nor did Holstius ask for his mediation any longer, being satisfied that he had got from the girl all the friendship which she had to offer.

The other two suitors, who would not be denied, but returned continually, were of coarser mould. They belonged to the very extensive class of men who, because they desire a thing vehemently, think themselves ill-used if they do not get it, fly into rages, accuse Providence, curse the hour of their birth, and go distraught. Sometimes, as in the case of the young Frenchman whose story is treated by Robert Browning, they throw themselves into the Seine, and so an end, because the joys of this world are denied to the poor. At other times they go about glaring with envious and malignant eyes. At all times they are the enemies of honest Christian folk.

One of these men was Captain Nicolas Borlinder, whose ship sailed to and fro from Calais to

the Port of London, carrying casks of sherry for
the thirsty British aristocracy.   It is not a highly-
paid service, and culture of the best kind is not
often found among the captains in that trade.
Yet Nick Borlinder was a happy man, because his
standard was of a kind easily attainable.   Like his
friends of the same service, he loved beer, rum,
and tobacco ; like them he loved these things in
large quantities ; like them he delighted to sit and
tell yarns.   He could also sing a good song in a
coarse baritone ; he could dance a hornpipe—
only among brother captains, of course—as well
as any fo'k'sle hand ; and he had the reputation
of being a smart sailor. This reputation, however,
belonged to all.

It was an unlucky day for Lal when this man
was allowed a right of entry to Rydquist's.   For
he immediately fell in love with her and resolved
to make her his own—Mrs. Borlinder—which
would have been fine promotion for her.

He was a red-faced, jolly-looking man of five
and thirty, or thereabouts.   He had a bluff and
hearty way ashore ; aboard ship he was handy
with a marlingspike, a rope's-end, a fist, a kick,
or a round, stimulating oath, or anything else
strong and rough and good for knocking down
the mutinous or quickening the indolent.   Behind
his hearty manner there lay—one can hardly say
concealed—a nature of the most profound selfish-

ness ; and it might have been remarked, had any of the captains been students of human nature, which is not a possible study, save on a very limited scale, for sailors, that among them all Nick Borlinder was about the only one who had no friends.

He came and went. When he appeared no one rejoiced ; while he stayed he sang and laughed and told yarns ; when he went away nobody cared.

Now, a skipper can go on very well as a bachelor up to the age of thirty-five or even forty. He is supported by the dignity and authority of his position ; he is sustained by a sense of his responsibilities ; perhaps, also, he still looks forward to another fling in port, for youthful follies are cherished and linger long in the breasts of sailors, and are sometimes dear even to the gravity of the captain. When a man reaches somewhere about thirty-five years of age, however, there generally comes to him a sense of loneliness. It seems hard that there should be no one glad to see him when he puts into port ; visions arise of a cottage with green palings and scarlet-runners, and, in most cases, that man is doomed when those visions arise.

Captain Borlinder was thirty-one or so when he first saw Lal. She was in her housekeeper's room making up accounts, and he brought her a letter from a 'Rydquist's man,' introducing him and requesting for him admission. She read the letter, asked him what his ship was, and where she traded, and showed him a room in her girlish, business-like manner. This was in the year eighteen hundred and seventy-six, shortly before she met Rex Armiger.

Captain Borlinder instantly, in her own room, at the very first interview, fell in love with her, and, like many men of his class, concluded that she was equally ready to fall in love with him.

All the next voyage out he thought about her. His experience of women was small, and of such a woman as Lal Rydquist, such a dainty maiden, he had no experience at all, because he had never known any such, or even distantly resembling her. The talk of such a girl, who could be friendly and laugh with a roomful of captains, and yet not one of them would dare so much as to chuck her under the chin—a delicate attention he had always heretofore allowed himself to consider proper—was a thing he had never before experienced. Then her figure, her face, her quickness, her cleverness—all these things excited his admiration and his envy. Should he allow such a treasure to be won by another man?

Then he thought of her business capacity and that snug and comfortable business at Rydquist's. What a retreat, what a charming retreat for him-

self, after his twenty years of bucketing about the
sea! He pictured himself a partner in that
business—sleeping partner, smoking partner,
drinking partner, the partner told off to narrate
the yarns and shove the bottle round. What a
place for a bluff, hearty, genuine old salt! How
richly had he deserved it!

He resolved, during that voyage, upon making
Lal Rydquist his own as soon as he returned.
They met with nasty weather in the Bay, and a
night or two on deck, which he had alway pre-
viously regarded as part of his profession and all
in the day's work, became a peg for discontent as
he thought of the snug lying he might have
beside—not in—the churchyard in the Seven
Houses.

The more he thought of the thing the more
clearly he saw, in his own mind, its manifest
advantages. And then, because the seclusion of
the cabin and the solitude of the captain's position
afford unrivalled opportunities for reflection, he
began to build up a castle of Spain, and pictured
to himself how he would reign as king-consort of
Rydquist's.

'The old woman,' he said, 'shall be the first
to go. No useless hands allowed aboard that
craft. Her room shall be mine, where I will
receive my own friends and count the money. As
for old Zachariasen, he may go too, if he likes

We shall get more by a succession of captains than by feeding him all the year round. And as for the feeding, it's too good for the money; they don't want such good grub. And the charges are too low; and the drinks ridiculous for cheapness. And as for Lal, she'd make any house go, with her pretty ways.'

About this point a certain anxiety crossed his mind, because the girl herself rather frightened him. In what terms should he convey his intentions? And how would she receive them?

When he got back to London he hastened to propose to Lal. He adopted the plain and hearty manner, with a gallant nautical attitude, indicating candour and loyalty. This manner he had studied and made his own. It was not unlike the British tar of the stage, except that the good old 'Shiver my timbers!' with the hitch-up of the trousers, went out before Nick Borlinder's time. Now it must be remembered that this was very shortly after young Armiger's departure.

'What you want, my hearty,' said Captain Borlinder, 'is a jolly husband, that's what you want; and the best husband you can have is a sailor.'

Lal was accustomed to propositions of this kind, though not always conveyed in language so downright, having already refused four and twenty captains, and laughed at half a dozen more, who lamented their previous marriages for her sake, and would have even seen themselves widowers with resignation.

'Why a sailor, Captain Borlinder?'

'Because a sailor is not always running after your heels like a tame cat and a puppy-dog. He goes to sea, and is out of sight; he leaves you the house to yourself; and when he comes home again he is always in a good temper. A sailor ashore is easy, contented, and happy-go-lucky.'

'It certainly would be something,' said Lal, 'always to have a good-tempered husband.'

'A sailor for me, says you,' continued the Captain, warming to his work. 'That's right; and if a sailor, quartermaster is better than able seaman; mate is better than quartermaster. Wherefore, skipper is better than mate; and if skipper, why not Nick Borlinder? Eh! Why not Nick Borlinder?'

And he stuck his thumbs in his waistcoat-pockets, and looked irresistible tenderness, so that he was greatly shocked when Lal laughed in his face, and informed him that she could not possibly become Mrs. Borlinder.

He went away in great indignation, and presently hearing about Rex Armiger and his successful courtship, first declared that he would break the neck of that young man as soon as he could get a chance, and then found fault with his own eyes because he had not struck at once and proposed when the idea first came into his head. Lost! and all for want of a little pluck. Lost! because the moment his back was turned, this young jackanapes, no better than a second mate in a steamer, cut in, saw his chance, and snapped her up.

For two voyages he reflected on the nature of women. He said to himself that out of sight, out of mind, and she would very likely forget all about the boy. He therefore resolved on trying the effect of bribery, and came offering rare gifts, consisting principally of an octave of sherry.

Lal accepted it graciously, and set it up in the Captains' room, where everybody fell to lapping it up until it was all gone.

Then Lal refused the donor a second time. So the sherry was clean thrown away and wasted. Much better had made it rum for his own consumption.

We know what happened next, and none rejoiced more cordially than Captain Borlinder over his rival's death.

When a reasonable time, as he thought, had elapsed, he renewed his offer with effusion, and was indignantly, even scornfully, refused. He concluded that he had another rival, probably some fellow with more money, and he looked about him and made more guarded enquiries. He could find no one likely to be a rival except Captain Holstius, who appeared to be a poor religious creature, not worth the jealousy of a lusty English sailor; and later on, he discovered that a certain American captain called Barnabas B. Wattles, who came and went, having no ship of his own, and yet always full of business, was certainly a rival.

Captain Wattles puzzled him, because, so far as he could see, Lal was no kinder to him than to himself. Always there was present to his mind that vision of himself the landlord or proprietor of Rydquist's, counting out the money in the front parlour over a pipe and a cool glass of rum-and-water, while Lal looked after the dinners and made out the bills.

'Bills!' he thought. 'Yes; they should be bills with a profit in them, too, when he was proprietor!'

Rage possessed his soul as the time went on and he got no nearer the attainment of his object. He could not converse with the girl, partly because she avoided him, and partly because he had nothing to say. Worst of all, she told him when he ventured once more to remark that a jolly sailor—namely, Nick Borlinder—would restore her to happiness, that if he ever dare to propose such a thing again he would no longer be admitted to Rydquist's, but might stay aboard his own ship in the London Docks, or find a house at Poplar. Fear of being sent to Poplar kept him quiet.

There remained the third suitor, Captain Barnabas B. Wattles.

When he made the acquaintance of Lal, a skipper without a ship, it was in the year eighteen hundred and seventy-seven. He was an American by birth, hailing, in fact, from the town of Portsmouth, New Hampshire, and he was always full of business, the nature of which no man knew. He was quite unlike the jovial Nick Borlinder, and indeed, resembled the typical British tar in no respect whatever. For he was a slight, spare man, with sharp features and hairless cheek. He was not, certainly, admitted to the privileges of Rydquist's, but he visited when his business brought him to London, and sat of an evening in the Captains' room drinking with anyone who would offer gratuitous grog; at other times he was fond of saying that he was a temperance man, and went away without grog rather than pay for it himself.

He first came when Lal was waiting for that letter from Rex which never came. He learned the whole story; and either did not immediately fall in love, like the more inflammable Borlinder, being a man of prudence and forethought, else he refrained from speech, even from the good words of courtship. But he came often; by speaking gently, and without mention of love and marriage, he established friendly relations with Lal; he even ventured to speak of her loss, and, with honeyed sympathy, told the tales of like disasters, which always ended fatally to American sailors. When she declared that Rex could not be drowned, he only shook his head with pity. And, in speaking of those early deaths at sea which had come under his own observation, he assumed as a matter of course, that the bereaved woman mourned for no more than a certain term, after which time she took unto herself another sweetheart, and enjoyed perfect happiness ever afterwards. He thought that in this way he would familiarise her mind with the idea of giving up her grief.

'When she reflected,' he would conclude his narrative, ' that cryin' would not bring back any man to life again, she gave over cryin' and looked about for consolation. She found it, Miss Lal, in the usual quarter. As for myself, my own name is Barnabas, which means, as perhaps you have never heard,. the Son of Consolation.'

With such words did he essay to sap the fidelity of the mourner, but in vain, for though there were times when poor Lal would doubt, despite the fervent ardour of her faith, whether

Rex might not be really dead and gone, there was no time at all when she ever wavered for a moment in constancy to his memory. Though neither Borlinder or Barnabas Wattles could understand the thing, it was impossible for Lal ever to think of a second lover.

He would talk of other things, but always came back to the subject of consolation.

Thus one evening he began to look about him, being then in her own room.

'This,' he said, 'is a prosperous concern which you are running, Miss Lal. I guess it pays?'

Yes; Lal said that it paid its expenses, and more.

'And you've made your little pile already out of it?'

Yes, said Lal, carelessly, there was money saved.

His eyes twinkled at the thought of handling her savings, for Captain Wattles was by no means rich. He forgot, however, that the money belonged to her mother.

'Now,' he went on, with an insinuating smile, 'do you never think the time will come when you will tire of running this ho—tel?'

Lal said she was too busy to think of what might happen, and that, as regards the future, she said, sadly, she would rather not think about

it at all, the past was already too much for her to
think about.

'Yes,' he said, 'that time will come. It has
not come yet, Miss Lal, and, therefore, I do not
say, as I am ready to say, Take me and let
me console you. My name is Barnabas, which
means, as perhaps you do not know, the Son of
Consolation.'

'It would be no use at all,' said Lal; 'and if
we are to remain friends, Captain Wattles, you
will never speak of this again.'

'I will not,' he replied, 'until the right
moment. Then, with your little savings and
mine, we will go back to the States. I know
what we will do when we get there. There's an
old ship-building yard at Portsmouth which
only wants a few thousand dollars put into it. We
will put our dollars into that yard, and we will
build ships.'

'You had better give up thinking of such
nonsense,' said Lal.

'Thought is free, Miss Lal. The time will
come. Is it in nature to go on crying all your
life for a man as dead as Abraham Lincoln? The
time will come.'

'Enough said, Captain Wattles,' Lal said. It
was in her own room, and she was busy with her
accounts. 'You can go now, and you need not
come back any more unless you have something

else to say. I thought you were a sensible man.
Most American captains I know are as sensible as
Englishmen and Norwegians.'

Captain Wattles rose slowly.

'Wal,' he said, 'you say so now. I expected
you would. But the time will come. I'm not
afraid of the other men. As for Cap'en Borlinder,
he is not fit company for a sweet young thing
like you. He would beat his wife, after a while,
that man would. He drinks nobblers all day,
and swaps lies with any riff-raff who will stand in
a bar and listen to him. You will not lower
yourself to Cap'en Borlinder. As for the Norweegee, he is but a poor soft shell; you might as
well marry a gell. I shan't ask you yet, so don't
be afraid. When your old friends drop away one
by one, and you feel a bit lonesome with no one
to talk to, and these bills always on your mind,
and the house over your head like a cage and a
prison, I shall look in again, and you will hold
out your pretty hand, and you will sweetly say:
"Cap'en Wattles, you air a sailor and a temperance man; you subscribe to a missionary society
and have once been teacher in a Sunday-school;
you have traded Bibles with natives for coral and
ivory and gold-dust; you air smart; you air
likewise a kind-hearted man, who will give his
wife her head in everything, with Paris bonnets
and New York frocks; your name is Barnabas

the Son of Consolation." . . . Don't run away,
Miss Lal. I've said all I wanted to say, and now
I am going. Business takes me to Liverpool
to-night, and on Thursday I sail again for
Baltimore.'

CHAPTER VI.

THE MESSAGE FROM THE SEA.

IT was, then, in October, eighteen hundred and seventy-nine, that Dick, the Malay, made his appearance and told his tale. Having told it he remained in the house, attaching himself as by right to Lal, whose steward he became as he had been steward to Rex.

The thing produced, naturally, a profound sensation in the Captains' room, whither Dick was invited to repeat his performance, not once, but several times.

It was observed that, though substantially the same, the action always differed in the addition or the withdrawal of certain small details, the interpretation of which was obscure. One or two facts remained certain, and were agreed upon by all : an open boat, a long waiting, a rescue, either by being picked up or by finding land, and then one or two fights, but why, and with whom, was a matter of speculation.

Captain Zachariasen remained obstinate to his

theory. There was a widow, there was a marriage, there was a baby, there were conjugal rows, and finally a prison in which Rex Armiger still remained. How to fit the pantomime into these wonderful details was a matter of difficulty which he was always endeavouring to overcome by the help of the more obscure gestures in the mummicking.

The general cheerfulness of the house was naturally much elevated by this event. It was, indeed, felt not only that hope had returned, but also that honour was conferred upon Rydquist's by so mysterious and exciting a revelation.

This distinction became more generally recognised when the Secretary and one of the Directors of the Indian Peninsular Line came over to see the Malay, hoping to get some light thrown upon the loss of their ship.

Captain Zachariasen took the chair for the performance, so to speak, and expounded the principal parts, taking credit for such mummicking as no other house could offer.

The Director learned nothing definite from the pantomime, but came away profoundly impressed with the belief that their officer, Captain Armiger, was living.

The Malay, now domesticated at Seven Houses, was frequently invited of an evening to the Captains' room, where he went through his performance—Captain Zachariasen always in the chair—for every new comer, and was a continual subject of discussion. Also there were great studyings of charts, and mappings out of routes, with calculations as to days and probable number of knots. And those who had been in Chinese and Polynesian waters were called upon to narrate their experiences.

The route of a steamer from Hong-Kong to Moreton Bay is well known, and easily followed. Unfortunately, the Malay's pantomime left it doubtful of what nature was the disaster. It might have been a piratical attack, though that was very unlikely, or a fire on board, or the striking on a reef.

' Her course,' said Captain Holstius, laying it down with Lal for the fiftieth time, ' would be— so—E.S.E. from Hong-Kong, north of Luçon here; then due S E. between the Pelews and Carolines, through Dampier Straits, having New Guinea to the starboard. Look at these seas, Lal. Who knows what may have happened? And how can we search for him over three thousand miles of sea, among so many islands? '

How, indeed? And yet the idea was growing up strong in both their minds that a search of some kind must be made.

And then came help, that sort of help which our pious ancestors called Providential. What can we call it? Blind chance? That seems rather a long drop from benevolent Providence, but it seems to suit a good many people nowadays almost as well—more's the pity.

Two months after the Malay's appearance, while winter was upon us and Christmas not far off, when the churchyard trees were stripped of leaf, and the vine about the window was trimmed, the garden swept up for the season, and the parrots brought indoors, and Rydquist's made snug for bad weather, another person called at the house, bringing with him a message of another kind. It was no other than the Doctor of the 'Aryan,' Rex's old ship. He bore something round, wrapped in tissue paper. He carried it with great care, as if it was something very precious.

The time was evening, and Lal was in her room making up accounts. In the Captains' room was a full assemblage, numbering Captain Zachariasan, Captain Borlinder, who purposed to spend his Christmas at Rydquist's and to consume much grog, Captain Holstius, Captain Barnabas B. Wattles, whose business had again brought him to London, and two or three captains who have nothing to do with this history except to fill up the group in the room where presently an important Function was to be held.

At present they were unsuspicious of what

was coming, and they sat in solemn circle, the Patriarch at the head of the table, getting through the evening, all too quickly, in the usual way.

'This was picked up,' the Doctor said, still holding his treasure in his hands as if it was a baby, 'in the Bay of Bengal, by a country ship sailing from Calcutta to Moulmein; it must have drifted with the currents and the wind, two thousand miles and more. How it contrived never to get driven ashore or broken against some boat, or wreck, or rock, or washed up some creek among the thousands of islands by which it floated, is a truly wonderful thing.'

'Oh, what is it?' she cried.

He took off the handkerchief and showed a common wide-mouthed bottle, such as chemists use for effervescing things.

'It contains,' he said, solemnly, 'poor Rex Armiger's last letter to you. The skipper who picked it up pulled out the cork and read it. He brought it to our office at Calcutta, where, though it was written to you, we were obliged to read it, because it told how the "Philippine" was cast away; for the same reason our officers read it.'

'His last letter?'

'Yes; his last letter. It is dated three years ago. We cannot hope—no, it is impossible to hope—that he is still alive. We should have heard long ago if he had been picked up.'

'We have heard,' said Lal. She went in search of the Malay, with whom she presently returned. 'We have heard, Doctor. Here is Rex's steward, who came to us two months ago.'

'Good heavens! it is the dumb Malay steward, who was with him in the boat.'

'Yes. Now look, and tell me what you read.'

She made a sign to Dick, who went through, for the Doctor's instruction, the now familiar pantomime.

'What do you think, Doctor?'

'Think? There is only one thing to think, Miss Rydquist. He has escaped. He is alive, somewhere, or was when Dick last saw him, though how this fellow got away from him, and where he is——'

'Now give me his letter.'

It was tied round with a green ribbon—a slender roll of paper, looking as if sea-water had discoloured it.

The Doctor took it out of the bottle and gave it her.

'I will read Rex's letter,' she said, quietly, 'alone. Will you wait a little for me, Doctor?'

She came back in a quarter of an hour. Her eyes were heavy with tears, but she was calm and assured.

'I thank God, Doctor,' she said; 'I thank God most humbly for preserving this precious bottle and this letter of my dear Rex—my poor

Rex—and I thank you, too, and your brother-officers, whom he loved, and who were always good to him, for bringing it home to me. For now I know where he is, and where to look for him, and now I understand it all.'

'If he is living we will find him,' said the Doctor. 'Be sure that we will find him.'

'We will find him,' she echoed. 'Yes, we will find him. Now, Doctor, consider. You remember how they got into the boat?'

'Yes—off the wreck. The letter tells us that.'

'Dick told us that two months ago, but we could not altogether understand it. How long were they in the boat?'

'Why, no one knows.'

'Yes, Dick knows, and he has told us. Consider. They were left, when this bottle was sent forth like the raven out of the ark, with no food. They sat in the boat, waiting for death. But they did not die. They drifted—you saw that they made no attempt to row—for awhile; they grew hungry and thirsty; they passed two or three days with nothing to eat. It could not have been more, because they were not so far exhausted but that, when land appeared in sight, they still had strength to row.'

'Go on,' cried the Doctor. 'You are cleverer than all of us.'

'It is because I love him,' she replied, ' and

because I have thought day and night where he can be. You know the latitude and longitude of the wreck; you must allow for currents and wind; you know how many days elapsed between the wreck and the writing of the letter. Now let us look at the chart and work it all out.'

She brought the chart to the table, and pointed with her finger.

'They were wrecked,' she said, 'there. Now allow five days for drifting. Where would they land? Remember he says that the wind was S.W.'

'Why,' said the Doctor, 'they may have landed on one of the most westerly of the Caroline Islands, unless the current carried them to the Pelews. There are islands enough in those seas.';

'Yes,' she replied; 'it is here that we shall look for him. Now come with me to the Captains' room.'

She walked in, head erect and paper in hand, followed by the Doctor, and stood at Captain Zachariasen's right—her usual place when she visited the captains in the evening.

'You, who are my friends,' said Lal, bearing in one hand the chart and in the other the precious letter, 'will rejoice with me, for I have had a letter from Rex.'

'When was it wrote and where from?' asked Captain Zachariasen.

'It is nearly three years old. It has been tossing on the sea, driven hither and thither, and preserved by kind Heaven to show that Rex is living still, and where he is.'

Captain Wattles whistled gently. It sounded like an involuntary note of incredulity.

Lal spread the chart before Captain Zachariasen.

'You can follow the voyage,' she said, 'while I read you this letter. It is on the back of one from me. It is written with a lead pencil, very small, because he had a great deal to say and not much space to say it in—my Rex!'

Her voice broke down for a moment, but she steadied herself and went on reading the message from the sea.

' " Anyone who picks this up," it begins, " will oblige me by sending it to Miss Rydquist, Seven Houses, Rotherhithe, because it tells her of the shipwreck and perhaps the death "—But you know, all of you,' Lal interposed, ' that he survived and got to land, else how was Dick able to get to England?—" of her sweetheart, the undersigned Rex Armiger, Captain of the steamer ' Philippine,' now lying a wreck on a reef in latitude 5·30 N. and longitude 133·25, as near as I could calculate."

' " MY DEAREST LAL,—I write this in the captain's gig, where I am floating about in or about the above-named latitude and longitude, after the most unfortunate voyage that ever started with good promise. First, I send you my last words, dear love, solemnly, because a man in a boat on the open seas, with no provisions and no sail, cannot look for anything but death from starvation, if not by drowning. God help you, my dear, and bless you, and make you forget me soon, and find a better husband than I should ever have made. You will take another man——"'

'Hear, hear!' said Captain Borlinder, softly.

'Hush!' said Captain Wattles, reproachfully. 'Captain Armiger was a good man and a prophet.'

' "You will take another man," ' Lal repeated. 'Never!' she cried, after the repetition, looking from one to the other, 'Never! Not if he were dead, instead of being alive, as he is, and wondering why we do not come to rescue him.'

'The boy had his points,' said Captain Zachariasen, 'and a good husband he would have made. Just such as I was sixty years ago, or thereabouts. Get on to the shipwreck, Lal, my dear.'

' "It was on December the First that we set sail from Calcutta. The crew were all Lascars, except Dick, my Malay steward, the chief officer, who was an Englishman, and the engineer. We made a good passage under canvas, with auxiliary screw, to Singapore, and from thence, in ballast, except for a few bales of goods, to Hong-Kong. Here we took in our cargo of rice, and started, all well, on January the Fourteenth, eighteen hundred and seventy-seven. The mate was a good sailor as ever stepped on a bridge, and the ship well found, new, and good in all respects.

' " We had fair weather across the China Sea and in the straits north of Luçon until we came to the open seas. Here a gale, which blew us off our course to N.E., but not far, and still in clear and open sailing, with never a reef or an island on the chart. We kept steam up, running in the teeth of the wind, all sails furled. .When the wind moderated, veering from S.E. to S.W. (within a point or two), we made the Pelew Islands to the starboard bow, and came well in the track of the Sydney steamers. If you look at the chart you will find that here the sea is open and clear; not a shoal nor an island laid down for a good thousand miles. Wherefore, I make no doubt that after enquiry I should have my certificate returned to me, in spite of having lost so good a ship.

' " On Sunday, at noon, the wind having moderated, we found we had made two hundred and twenty-seven knots in four and twenty hours. We were, as I made it, in latitude 5·30 N. and longitude 133·25, as near as I could calculate. At sunset, which was at six twenty-five, we must have made some sixty miles more to the S.W., so that you can lay down the spot on the map. The wind was fresh, and the sea a little choppy, but nothing of any consequence in open water. At eight I turned in, going watch and watch about with the mate, and at five minutes past eight, I suppose I was fast asleep.

' " It was, I think, a little after six bells, that I was awakened by the ship striking. I ran on deck at once. We were on a reef, and by the grating and the grinding of her bottom I guessed that it was all over. I'm sorry to say that in the shock the mate seems to have been knocked overboard and drowned, because I saw him no more. The ship rolled from side to side, grinding and tearing her bottom upon the reef. The men ran backwards and forwards crying to each other. There was no discipline with them, nor could I get them to obey orders. The engineer went below and reported water gaining fast. He and I did our best to keep the crew in hand; but it was no use. They lowered the boats and pushed off leaving behind only the engineer, and Dick the steward, and myself. They were in too great a hurry to put provisions on board, so that I greatly fear they must have perished, unless they have been picked up by some steamer.

' " All that night we stayed on deck, we three, expecting every moment that she would break her back. The cargo of grain was loose now, and rolled with the ship like water. Her bows were high upon the rocks, and I believe we were only saved because she was lodged upon the reef as far aft as the engine-room. In the darkness the engineer must have slipped his hold and fallen overboard, I don't know how. Then there was only Dick and me.

' " In the morning, at daybreak, the look-out was pretty bad. The reef is a shoal, with nothing but a fringe of white water round it to mark where it lies. It is now, I reckon, about seventeen feet below the surface of the water, but I take it to be a rising reef, so that every year will make it less, and I hope it will be set down at once on the chart. My mate was gone and my engineer, the boats and their crews were out of sight, or, may be, capsized, not a sail upon the sea. But there was the captain's gig.

' " When we got afloat, my purpose was to keep alongside the poor wreck until we had got enough victuals to last a week or two, and some running tackle whereby we could hoist some sort of a sail. But, my dear, we hadn't time, because no sooner had we lowered the boat and put in a few tins, with a bottle half full of brandy and a keg of water, than she parted amidships, and we had no more than time to jump into the boat and shove off.

' " There we were, then, with no oars, no mast, no sail, no rudder even, and provisions for two or three days.

' " We have now been floating a week. We drifted first of all in a nor'-westerly direction, so near as I could make out, so long as the poor wreck remained in sight. Since then I know not what our course has been. There is a strong current here, I suspect, from the short time we took to lose sight of her, and there has been a good breeze blowing from the S.W. for three days.

' " We have now got to the end of our provisions; the last drop of water has been drunk; the last biscuit eaten. Poor Dick sits opposite to me all day and all night, he cannot speak, but he refused his share of the last ration for my sake.'

Here Lal broke down again, and Captain Zachariasen said something strong, which showed that his admiration for a generous action was greater than his religious restraint.

' " We spend the day in looking for a sail; at night we take watch about. There remains only a little brandy in the heel of the bottle. We husband that for a last resource. We have fashioned a couple of rough oars out of two planks of the boat.

' " I have kept this a day longer. No sail in sight. We have had two or three drops of brandy each. They are the last. Now I must commit this letter to the sea in the bottle. Oh, my dear Lal, my pretty, tender darling! I shall never, never see you any more. Long before you get this letter I shall be drifting about in this boat a dead man. I pray Heaven to bless you——" '

Here Lal stopped and burst into tears.

'Read no more,' said Captain Holstius, 'the rest concerns yourself alone.'

Lal kissed her letter, folded it tenderly, and laid it in her bosom.

'The rest only concerns me,' she repeated, and was silent awhile.

Captain Zachariasen, meantime, was at work upon the chart.

'I read this story somewhat different,' he said. 'You can't always follow a mummicker in his antics, and I now perceive that I was wrong about the baby. The widow I stick to. Nothing could be plainer than the widow, though, of course, it was not to be expected that he'd make a clean breast of it in that letter, which otherwise does him credit. Lal, my dear, you are right. If Dick is alive, then his master is alive. Question is, where would he get to, and where is he now?'

They were all silent, waiting the conclusion of the Patriarch before any other ventured to speak. He was bending over the chart, his right thumb

as the position of the reef, and his fore-finger
acting as a compass.

'I calculate from the position of the reef,
which is here, and the run of the currents, and
the direction of the wind, that they drifted
towards the most westerly of the Caroline Islands.'

It hardly required patriarchal wisdom to sur-
mise this fact, seeing that these islands are the
nearest places north-west of the reef.

'And next?' asked Lal.

'Next, my pretty, they were taken off of that
island, but I do not know by whom, and were
shipped away to some prison, but I don't know
where, and there Cap'en Armiger is still lying,
though what for, as there was seemingly no baby
and no chucking overboard, we mortals, who are
but purblind, cannot say.'

Then Captain Holstius spoke again.

'I think we might have in the Malay and go
through the play acting again. May be, with this
letter before us, we may get more light.'

The Doctor now showed Dick the bottle.
He seized it, grinned a recognition, and, on a
sign from the girl, began the story again at that
point.

First, leaning over the imaginary side of the
boat, he laid it gently on the floor.

'Thereby,' said Captain Zachariasen, solemnly,
'committing the letter to the watery deep, to be

carried here and driven there while the stormy winds do blow, do blow.   Amen!'

Then Dick became pensive.   He sat huddled up, with his elbows on his knees and his head in his hands, looking straight before him.   For the time, as always in this performance, of which he never tired, he was Rex himself; the same poise of the head, the same look of the eyes; he had put off the Malayan type, and sat there, before them all, pure Caucasian.

'Creditable, my lad,' said Captain Zachariasen. 'I think you can, all of you, understand so far, without my telling.'

They certainly could.

Then the Malay sprang to his feet and pointed to some object in the distance.

'Sail ho!' cried Captain Borlinder.

Then he sat down again and began the regular motion of his arm, which the Patriarch had mistaken for rocking the baby.

'This,' said the Venerable, 'is plain and easy. Land it is, not a sail—why?   Because, if the latter, they would wave their pocket-handkerchiefs; if the former, they would h'ist sail or out sculls.   If the mummicker had been as plain and easy to understand the first time, we shouldn't have gone astray and sailed on that wrong tack about the baby.'

With the help of the letter the pantomime

became perfectly intelligible. The whole scene stood out plainly before the eyes of all. They were no longer in the Captains' room at Seven Houses, Rotherhithe; they were somewhere far away, east of New Guinea, watching two men in a little boat on a sea where there was no sail nor any smoke from passing steamers. Low down on the horizon was a thin streak, which a landsman would have taken for a cloud. The two men with straining faces were rowing with feverish eagerness, encouraging each other, and ceasing not, though the paddles nearly fell from their hands with fatigue.

'Oh! Rex, Rex!' cried Lal, carried away by the acting. 'Rest awhile; oh, rest!'

But still they paddled on.

Then came the scene of the struggle and the binding of the arms, and the march up country. Next the release and the quiet going up and down; and then the second struggle, with another capture, and a second binding of arms.

'See, Lal,' said Captain Holstius, pointing triumphantly to the actor; 'who is bound this time?'

Why, there could be no doubt whatever. It was not Rex, but the Malay.

'This is the worst o' mummicking now,' said the Patriarch, as if pantomime was a recognised instrument in the teaching and illustration of history. 'You're never quite sure. We've had to give up the baby with the chucking overboard. I was sorry for that, because it was so plain and easy to read. And now it seems as if it was the poor devil himself that got took off to gaol. Was his hair cut short, do you remember, Lal, when he came here two months ago? I can't quite give up the prison, neither, so beautiful as it reeled itself out first time we did the mummicking. You're a stranger, sir,' he addressed the Doctor, 'and you knew Cap'en Armiger. What do you think? For my own part—well, let's hear you, sir.'

'There cannot be a doubt,' said the Doctor, 'that the man personated Armiger, and no other, until the last scene, and that there he became himself intentionally. He exaggerated himself. He walked differently; he carried his head differently. There was a fight of some kind, and the Malay, not Armiger at all, was taken prisoner.'

'What is your opinion, Captain Borlinder?' asked Lal, anxious to know what each man thought.

'My opinion,' said Captain Borlinder, with emphasis, ' is this. They got ashore; no one can doubt that. Very well, then. Where? Not many degrees of longitude from the place where they were wrecked. Who were the people they fell among? The natives. That's what I read so

far.　Now we go on to the fight at the end.　A
better fight I never saw on the stage, not even at
the Pavilion Theatre, though but one man in it.
As for Captain Armiger, he was knocked on the
head.　That is to me quite certain.　Knocked on
the head with a stick, or stuck with a knife, according to the religion and customs of them
natives, among whom I never sailed, and therefore do not know their ways.　It's a melancholy
comfort, at all events, to know the manner of his
end.　Next to looking forward to a decent burial,
people when they are going to be knocked on the
head die more comfortable if they know that
other people will hear how they came to be
knocked on the head—whether a club, or a boat-
hook, or a bo'sn's cutlash.'

'I think, sir,' said the Doctor, ' that you are
perfectly wrong.　There is nothing whatever to
show that Armiger was killed.'

But then he did not know that Captain Borlinder spoke according to the desire of his own
heart.

Then Lal turned to the only man who had not
yet spoken :

' And what is your opinion, Captain Wattles?'

' I think,' replied Barnabas the Consoler, ' that
Cap'en Armiger landed on some island, and
worried through the first scrimmage.　I know
them lands, and I know that their ways to

strangers may be rough. If you get through the first hearty welcome, which means clubs and knives and spears mostly, there's no reason why you shouldn't settle down among 'em. There's many an English and American sailor living there contented and happy. P'raps Cap'en Armiger is one of them.'

'Not contented,' said Lal, 'nor yet happy.'

Captain Wattles went on :

'On the other hand, there's fights among themselves and drunken bouts, and many a brave fellow knocked on the head thereby.'

'Do you speak from you own knowledge?' asked the Doctor.

'I was once,' he replied, unblushingly, 'a missionary in the Kusaic station. Yes, we disseminated amongst us the seeds of civilisation and religion among those poor cannibals. I also traded in shirts and trousers, after they had been taught how to put them on. They are a treacherous race ; they treasure up the recollection of wrongs and take revenge ; they are insensible to kindness and handy with their arrows. I fear that Cap'en Armiger has long since been killed and eaten. They probably spared the Malay on account of his brown skin, as likely to disagree.'

Then Captain Holstius rose and spoke.

'Friends all,' he said, 'and especially Captain Borlinder and Captain Wattles, here is a message come straight from Captain Armiger himself, though now nigh upon three years old. And it comes close upon the heels of that other message brought us by this poor fellow who gave it as he knew best, though a difficult message to read in parts. Now we know, partly from Dick and partly from the letter, what happened and how it happened, and we are pretty certain that they must have landed, as Captain Zachariasen has told us, in one of the islands lying to the nor'-west of the spot where she struck.' Here he paused. Captain Borlinder blew great clouds of tobacco and looked straight before him. Captain Wattles listened with impatience. Then the Norwegian went on: 'I think, friends all, that here we have our duty plain before us. Here are three men in this room, Captain Borlinder, Captain Wattles, and myself, who have been in love with Lal, who is Captain Armiger's sweetheart, and therefore has no right to listen to us so long as there is any hope that he is alive. If no hope, why, I do not say myself that she has no right——'

'No right, Captain Holstius,' said Lal; 'no right to listen to any other man, whatever happens.'

'Very well, then. But for us who love her in a respectful way, and desire nothing but her happiness, there is only one duty, and that is——'

Here Captain Wattles sprang to his feet.

'To go in search of him. That is what I was going to propose. Miss Rydquist, I promise to go in search of Cap'en Armiger. If he is alive I will bring him home to you. If he is dead, I will bring you news of how and when he died. I ask no reward. I leave that to you. But I will bring you news.'

This was honestly and even nobly spoken. But the effect of the speech was a little marred by the allusion to reward. What reward had Lal to offer, except one? and she had just declared that to be impossible.

Then Captain Borlinder rose, ponderously, and slapped his chest.

'Nick Borlinder, Lal, is at your service. Yours truly to command. He hasn't been a missionary, nor a dealer in reach-me-down shirts, like some skippers, having walked the deck since a boy. And he doesn't know the Caroline Islands. But he can navigate a ship, or he can take a passage aboard a ship. Where there's missionaries there's ships. He will get aboard one of them ships, and he will visit those cannibals and find out the truth. Lal, if Cap'en Armiger is alive, he shall be rescued by Nick Borlinder, and shall come home with me arm-in-arm to the Pride of Rotherhithe. If he isn't alive, why— then——'

He sat down again, nodding his head.

Lal turned to Captain Holstius.

'Yes,' he said; 'I thought this brave Englishman and this brave American would see their duty plain before them. I will go in search of him, too, Lal. I know not yet how; but I shall find a way.'

'Gentlemen,' said Lal, ' I have nothing to give you except my gratitude. Nothing at all. Oh! who in the world has ever had kinder and nobler friends than I ? '

She held out her two hands. Captain Wattles seized the right and kissed it with effusion, murmuring something about Barnabas, the Son of Consolation. Captain Borlinder followed his example with the left, though he had never before regarded a woman's hand as a proper object for a manly kiss. He took the opportunity to whisper that, in all her troubles, Nick Borlinder was the man to trust.

'Now,' said Captain Holstius, 'there is no time to be lost; we all have things to arrange, and money to raise. Shall we all go together, or shall we go separate ? '

'Separate,' said the Son of Consolation.

'Separate,' cried Borlinder, firmly. 'If the job is to be done, let ME do the job single-handed.'

'Very well,' said Captain Holstius ; ' then how shall we go ? '

' We will go,' said Captain Wattles, ' in order. First one, and then another, to give every man a fair chance and no favour. And to get that fair chance we will draw straws. Longest straw first, shortest last.'

He retired and returned with three straws in his hand.

'Now, Borlinder,' he said, 'you shall draw first.'

Borlinder took a straw, but with hesitation.

The Doctor, who was rather short-sighted, thought he detected a little sleight-of-hand on the part of Captain Wattles at this moment. But he said nothing. Captain Holstius then drew. Again the Doctor thought he observed what seemed to be tampering with the oracle of the straw.

On the display of the straws it was found that the longest straw was Captain Borlinder's; the shortest, that of Captain Holstius. The order of search was therefore, first, Captain Borlinder. He heaved a great breath, struck his hands together, and smote his chest with great violence and heartiness. You would have thought he had drawn a great prize instead of the right to go first on an extremely expensive voyage of search. The next was to be Captain Wattles. The third and last, Captain Holstius.

Captain Zachariasen called for glasses round

to drink health and success to the gallant fellows going out on this brave and honourable quest.

Outside the house, presently, two of the gallant seekers stood in discourse.

'You don't think, Wattles,' asked Borlinder, 'that he's really alive?'

'I can't say,' replied the ex-missionary. 'I shouldn't like, myself, to be wrecked on one of those islands. You see, there's been a little labour traffic in those parts, and the ungrateful people, who don't know what's good for them, are afraid of being kid— I mean recruited. And they bear malice. But I suppose he's one of the sort that don't easily get killed. I shall be going Sydney-way about my own business next year, or thereabouts, I expect, so it's all in my day's work to make enquiries. As for you——'

'As to me, now, brother?' Captain Borlinder spoke in his most insinuating way. 'As to me, now? Come, let's have a drink.'

'As to you,' said the Consoler, after a drink at his friend's expense, 'I'm sorry for you, because you've got to go at once, and you've got no experience. Among cannibals, a man of your flesh is like a prize ox at Christmas.'

Captain Borlinder turned pale.

'Yes—that is so. They would put you in a shallow pit, with a few onions and some pepper, cover all up snug with stones, and make a fire on top till you were done to a turn!'

Captain Borlinder shuddered.

'You are going first, you are, like a brave Briton. I will tell you a little story. There was once a man who promised to go over Niagara in an india-rubber machine of his own invention. A beautiful machine it was, shut up tight, with air-holes so as the man inside could breathe free and open when so disposed.'

'Well?'

'Wal, sir, he was cert'n'y bound to go. But after looking at the Falls a bit, he concluded to send a cat over first.'

'Well?'

'Yes, Cap'en Borlinder, the cat went over and that man is still waiting below the Horseshoe Fall for the critter to turn up again.'

Captain Borlinder looked after his friend with pale cheeks and apprehensive heart. What did it mean—this parable of the cat and Niagara?

Now, after the glass round was drank, and the three men gone, the Doctor found his way round the table and looked under it on the floor, and there found two short bits of straw lying on the carpet. He picked them up and considered. 'What did he do it for?' he asked. 'Longest first. They were, I suppose all the same length,

so that the man with the red face should go first.
Easy then, to nip bits off the straw and make the
Norway man take the shortest. What did he do
it for?' And the knowledge of this fact made
him uneasy, because it looked as if the search
for Armiger would not be altogether fair.

CHAPTER VII.

CAPTAIN BORLINDER AMONG THE CANNIBALS.

WHEN Captain Borlinder sought the privacy of his own chamber that evening, he gave way to meditations of a very unpleasant and exasperating nature. Was ever a man more forced into a hole than himself? Was ever proposition more ridiculous? Why, if, as Holstius truly said, they were all after the same girl, what the dickens was the good of going out of the country, all the way to the Eastern Seas, at enormous expense, to say nothing of the danger, in order to find and bring home the man who would cut them all out and carry the girl away? He would rather fight for the girl; he should like, he thought, to fight for the girl. That slow and easy Norweegee would pretty soon knock under, though the little Yankee would be more difficult to tackle. But actually to go and look for the man! Why, since he was happily disposed of, and if not dead, then missing for three years, what madness to disturb so comfortable and providential an arrangement!

As for such disinterestedness as to desire the happiness of any woman in the world as the first consideration, that was a thing too high for Nick Borlinder's understanding, a dark saying, a flight into unattainable heights, which appeared to him pure unmitigated nonsense. Should his own happiness, should any man's happiness, be wrecked to save that of any woman, or man either, on the whole earth? What is the happiness of another to a man who cannot himself be happy?

Who, thought honest Nicholas, without putting the thought into words, is the most important person, the central person, of the whole universe ; the person about whom the stars do revolve, for whom the sun shines and the rain falls, for whose protection governments exist, for whom all people who on earth do dwell continually toil, so that this person may receive good things without cessation? Who is it, but—*moi même*? Was, then, Captain Borlinder to labour and be spent for the promotion of another's happiness? Was he to give up his ship in order to find a man who would destroy his own best chance of good fortune? The thing appeared more preposterous every moment!

'Who, in fact,' he asked, giving full vent to his feelings, ' but a Norweegee could be such an enormous, such an incredible ass ? '

Then he remembered again the Yankee's apologue.

'Sniggerin' beast,' he said; 'I hate him! I wish he'd fall overboard of a dark night and blowin' great guns. What did he mean? I'm to be the cat to go over among the cannibals, am I?'

Then a beautiful and comforting thought crossed his mind.

'I know now,' he said, 'what I ought to have replied. I should have said there was a man cleverer than that man. For he promised to go over the Falls in a bathing-machine, or a sewing-machine, or a reaping-machine, or something, and he went away and presently he came back and said he'd done it.'

This happy repartee pleased him so much that he repeated it twice, and then sat down and thought it over with intentness.

'Why,' he said, to himself, reasoning as a Christian of the highest principle, ' man was told to stand out of the reach of temptation, and if I were to meet that man I might be tempted to knock him on the head. If it wasn't for Holstius and Wattles I would knock him on the head. But to kill a fellow for other fellows to reap the advantage of it, it doesn't seem quite worth while. Still, there's the temptation, and I oughtn't to go anigh of it. As for searching for him, again. Where am I to look for him? Am I to land on every island and pass the word for Cap'en Armiger? Naked black savages don't know about Cap'en Armiger. Ate him up, no doubt, long ago. Am I to put up a signal at every port for Cap'en Armiger? Do these ignorant natives know a signal when they see one? Very well, then. This Norweegee is all the bigger fool.'

As for the allegory of the cat, again. He was himself the cat. Pleasant thing for a man of his position to be compared to the cat which led the way over the Falls and was smashed and never returned again! Work that thing out as much as you please, and it always comes to this, that he, Nick Borlinder, was to go out first, get devoured by the cannibals, and never get back again.

Then the Yankee, himself out of the way, would try another way.

'I shan't go at all,' he murmured. 'Yah! for cheating and dishonesty give me a Yankee! I shall pretend to have been there!'

'As for finding him,' he went on, with his meditations, 'it's a thousand to one that you don't light on the island where he put foot ashore; and if you do find him, a million to one at least that he's dead—and all the journey, with the expense of it, for nothing.

'To say nothing of risk and danger. Shipwreck : I suppose that goes for nothing. Fever : I suppose we needn't reckon that. Oh, no, certainly not. Sunstroke : that never kills in tropical climates, does it ? Oh, no ; don't reckon that. Natives : they are a mild and dovelike race, ain't they ? Everybody knows that ! Don't reckon natives.'

It was, after all, very well to propose a pretended voyage, but what would the Yankee do ? And what did he really mean about the cat and the india-rubber ball ?

This doubt puzzled him not a little. The plan he proposed to himself was simple—beautiful in its simplicity. But he could not help feeling that his American cousin had some other and some deeper plan, by means of which he would himself be circumvented and anticipated.

Nothing more disturbs the crafty and subtle serpent, or more fills him with virtuous indignation, than the suspicion that his brother serpent is more crafty and more subtle than himself.

Everybody knows how the two burglars, friends in private but strangers in profession, met one night in the same house, proposing independent research.

His plan involved no expense, no danger, no possible privations. It was nothing more nor less than to wait awhile, and then to present himself with the report of a pretended voyage.

At first he thought he would so far give in to the outward seeming of things as to get a substitute to take command of his ship for a certain space, spending that time on shore in some secluded spot. This plan, however, involved a considerable amount of expense, with the necessity of much explanation to his employers. It therefore seemed to him best to go on just the same—to take his ship from the London Docks to Cadiz as usual, and back again, to give Rother-hithe a wide berth, and then, after a certain decent interval, to present himself at Seven Houses with a narrative.

Seven weeks to Hong-Kong, seven weeks back, eight weeks for the search—say six months in all.

Having roughly drawn out his plan of action, and considered in broad outlines the leading features of the narrative, Captain Borlinder purchased a few sheets of paper, on which to set down the account of his voyage, which he intended should be a masterly performance. He then, without waiting for the Christmas festivities, though nigh at hand—and no such pudding anywhere as at Rydquist's—presented himself at Rotherhithe to take farewell before he started on his long and dangerous journey.

This haste to redeem his promise could not fail, he thought, of producing a favourable impression.

He carried a red pocket-handkerchief, as if that contained all the luggage required for a hardy mariner even with such a journey before him. He had tied a string, with a jack-knife at the end of it, round his waist, like a common sailor. He had a profoundly shiny hat, and his face was set to an expression of as deep sympathy as he could command.

'I know,' he said, in his lowest tones, 'that to look for Cap'en Armiger in the Eastern Seas will very likely be a mighty tough job; but I've passèd my word to tackle that job, and when Nick Borlinder's word is passed to do a thing, that thing has got to be done, or the reason why is asked, pretty quick. Same as if I was in command of my own ship. For, sezi to myself, before ever the Norweegee up and spoke, or the Yankee pretended to have meant it—but I am slow to speak, though amazing quick to think— I sez, "What we three men have got to do in this business is to look after Lal's happiness." That I sez after you read that most affecting letter, before the talk begun, and speaking in a whisper, as a man might say, down his baccy-pipe. "Nothing else consarns us now. It is that which we have to look after. The way to look after it is to make quite sure that Cap'en

Armiger is gone, and the way he went, and where his remains remain ; or else, if he is not gone, but he still alive-and-kicks, wherever that may be, then to bring him home." '

'Thank you, Captain Borlinder,' said Lal, thinking that the Patriarch's dislike to this good and disinterested man was founded on prejudice ; and, indeed, the meaning was quite plain, though the language was a little mixed.

'There's a many islands in the Eastern Seas,' continued Nicholas the Brave. 'I've been looking at them in the charts. There's thousands of islands—say ten thousand, little and big. Say every one of those islands has to be searched. If we give a month to each island all round, counting little and big, that will make close upon nine hundred years. If it's only a fortnight, four hundred years. What's four hundred years to a determined man? I shall search among them islands, if it's four hundred or nine hundred years, till I find him.'

'But this will cost a great deal, Captain Borlinder, I am afraid.'

'Never mind about the cost,' he replied, grandly. 'If it was ten times as much I'd never grudge it. We will say good-bye now. 'Perhaps I shall come home, with news, in a year, or even less. Perhaps it may be forty years before I come home again. Perhaps I shall bring him home in a few months, well and hearty ; perhaps in about fifty years, with never a tooth to his head. But never you fear. Pluck up. Say to yourself : " Nick Borlinder, as never puts his hand to nothing but he carries that thing through, has got this job in hand." Perhaps I may come with news that you don't want. But there—we will not talk of that. If I never come home at all, but get, maybe, devoured by sharks, cannibals, and alligators, besides being struck with sun-stroke, fever, rheumatics, and other illnesses, and knocked on the head with clubs, and shot with poisoned arrows, so that there's an end, then, Lal, you will perhaps begin to think kind of a man who loved you so dear, that he went all that way alone to look for Cap'en Armiger, also with the Lord. For women never know the value of a man until he's gone.'

This said, he shook hands, wagging his head mournfully, but smiting his chest as if to repress the gloomy forebodings of his soul, and the manly sobs that choked further utterance.

Captain Holstius also went away, and Captain Wattles, who made no further allusion to the letter or the pledge he had made, also returned to Liverpool, whither, he said, business called him.

Then Lal was left alone with the letter of Rex to read and read again, and she never doubted that Captain Borlinder, true to his word, was on his way to the far East, to begin the search for her lost lover.

One man, however, doubted very much, but in a vague way. It was the Patriarch.

'Lal, my pretty,' he said, 'I mistrust two of them three chaps—the Yankee first, and Nick Borlinder next. As to Cap'en Wattles, he's told me over and over again that he wants to get back to the Pacific. It isn't hunting for Cap'en Armiger will take him back there. And as for Cap'en Borlinder, it's my opinion, my dear, that he means to make a voyage there and a voyage back, whereby to clear the cobwebs from his brain and the wrinkles from his eyes, and to gain experience. What then? Will either of them bring him back? Do they want him back? Think, my dear. No; they want him dead. The more dead he is the better they will be pleased. And if I was Cap'en Armiger, my pretty, and I was to see either of them brave master·mariners sailing up a creek with no one else in sight, I would sit snug, or I would prepare for a fight. My dear, they may talk, but they don't want him back! The only man who means honest is the Norweegee. As for him, he loves the very ground you tread upon, and I think he'd rather be your father than your husband, which, to be sure, was never a sailor's way when I was young ; and that, my dear, is seventy, and soon will be eighty, years ago: which proves the Fifth Commandment and shows how much I honoured my father and my mother—all the more because I never saw neither of them since ten years old.'

Captain Borlinder, dropping down the river on his next voyage, passed the Commercial Docks with a light and jocund heart. He was about to earn the gratitude of the girl he loved at a cheap rate—namely, at the cost of remaining out of her sight on the next occasion of his return to the Port of London. His love was not of that ardent and absorbing kind which prevents a man from feeling happy unless he is in the presence of the object of his affections. Quite the contrary. Captain Borlinder was happier away from the young lady, because conversation with her was carried on under considerable constraint. Once safely married, that constraint, he felt, would be removed, and expressions, now carefully guarded, might be again freely used. If a married man's house is not his own quarter-deck, what is it? thought the Captain, who, despite the culture of many centuries and the religion of his ancestors, retained the ideas of marital authority common among primitive men. He is now married, however, though not to Lal, and has learned to think quite otherwise.

The weather was favourable across the Bay,

and with all sail set, a rolling sea, and a fresh breeze, the Captain stood aft and began to consider the shaping of his narrative.

He was a good hand at a yarn. But then to write a yarn is, if you please, much more difficult than to spin one. The pen is a slow, tedious instrument. We want, in fact, something more rapid with which to interpret our thoughts. While we are painfully setting down one thing, the next, equally important, escapes us and is forgotten.

Captain Borlinder felt this, and therefore, very wisely, resolved upon not writing anything until he had thoroughly mastered the whole story and told it to himself half a dozen times over. Thus great novelists, I believe, get the whole of their situations clearly in their mind, with the grouping of the characters, before writing a word. And it would be an admirable plan if certain lady novelists would also follow the Captain's method, and write nothing before they are almost word-perfect with their story.

His crew were amazed at the behaviour of their skipper, both outward and homeward bound. For he paced the quarter-deck all day long, gazing at sky and sea. He struck strange attitudes; he shook his head; he swore at himself sometimes; he left the navigation of the ship to the mate; he seemed to be perpetually repeating words.

These things were strange. He was not drunk. He even seemed to drink less than usual; and, if he had got a touch of 'horrors,' as sometimes happens to sailors after a spell ashore, they were manifested in a most unusual manner.

On the voyage to Cadiz and back the Captain restricted himself to mental composition. We all know how difficult it is to describe a place which you have never seen. One would like to see a competitive young man's description, say of Rotherhithe, which nobody but myself has ever visited. That difficulty is, of course, lessened when your readers are equally ignorant, but immensely increased by the consideration that perhaps they know the place.

Now, certainly Lal had not seen any of the islands of Micronesia, or Polynesia. The contemplation of the chart whereon the countless islands of the Pacific lie dotted among the coral-reefs, the shoals, and atolls of that great sea, only filled her mind with vague thoughts of palm-trees, soft winds, and brown natives. In those seas sailed the ships she had heard of, the whalers, the schooners trading from island to island. On those dots of dry land lived men, of whom she had heard, who had grown grey in these latitudes, who cared no more to return to England, who had learned native ways and native customs. Though Lal had never travelled, she knew a great deal more than Captain Borlinder, and it might be embarrassing for him to be asked questions arising out of her superior knowledge.

Again, there was Captain Zachariasen. Nobody knew where that old man had not been in his long life of sixty years' sailing upon the sea. In his garrulous way, he laid claim to a knowledge of every port under the sun. Now, supposing he had actually visited the place fixed on by himself for the scene of Captain Armiger's exile and death. This, too, would be embarrassing.

It is true that Nick Borlinder was not one of those who place truth among the highest duties of mankind, but rather considered the search for enjoyment, in all its branches, as a duty immensely superior and, indeed, a duty to be ranked foremost among those imposed on suffering humanity. Yet the worst of lying is that you have got to be consistent in order to be believed. Random lying helps no man. It is a mere amusement, a display of cleverness, intellectual fireworks, the indulgence of imagination. The story, therefore, must be constructed in accordance, somehow, with possible facts.

The romancer had provided himself, not only with a few sheets of paper, but with a map, and over this he pored continually, seeking a likely spot for the scene of his Fabulous History. But it was not till his second return voyage that he found himself so far advanced with the story as to begin committing it to writing.

It is interesting to record further that the Captain on returning to London sought a book-seller's shop, and enquired after any work which treated of the Eastern Seas. He obtained a second-hand copy of an old book—I think by Captain Mundy—and then learned that the island of New Guinea, which he easily found on the map, was entirely unknown, and had hardly ever been visited. He therefore resolved to make New Guinea the scene of Rex Armiger's landing. At all events, Captain Zachariasen would be unable to put him to shame in the matter of New Guinea.

He made three voyages to and from Cadiz, bringing home a vast quantity of sherry, Portugal plums, raisins, oranges, and other things, and taking out I know not what, except that what he took out was not worth so much as what he brought home. And as this appears to be the case with every ship which leaves a British port, we must be working our way gaily through the national savings, and shall all very shortly take refuge in the national workhouse, so that the dreams of the Socialist will be realised, and all shall be on the same level. This is a very delight-ful prospect to contemplate, and the position of things reflects the highest credit on both sides of the House.

It was on October 14, 1879, that Dick, the Malay, came back and told his tale. It was in December following that the Doctor of the 'Aryan' brought the message from the sea. On January 2, Captain Borlinder took his farewell, and sallied forth on that desperate quest to the Eastern Seas, the description of which was written between Cadiz and London.

No news came to Rotherhithe all the winter. The 'Aryan' returned, and the Doctor came to say that the Company were making enquiries among the ships trading with the islands for news of a white man cast away upon one of them. No news had yet been received.

It was on June 8, 1880, that Captain Borlinder returned from the East.

He bore in his hand the same red silk pocket-handkerchief with which he had started, he wore the same blue clothes, in the same state of preservation, because they were his best; the same shiny hat.

He presented himself in the kitchen because it was in the forenoon, and Lal was engaged in her usual occupation—namely, the daily pudding. The Patriarch, as usual, sat in the armchair sound asleep.

She dropped her work and turned pale, seeing that he was alone.

'Alone!' she cried.

'Alone,' he answered, in the deepest and most sepulchral notes which his voice contained. 'Alone,' he repeated. 'I have been a long voyage, and have come back—alone. But not empty-handed. No; I have brought you news. Yes; bad news, I grieve to say.'

She sat down and folded her hands, prepared for the worst.

'Go on,' she said; 'tell me what you have to tell.'

At this juncture Captain Zachariasen awoke and rubbed his eyes.

'Ho! ho!' he said; 'here's one of them come back. Well, I thought he would be the first. What cheer, mate?'

'Bad,' replied the traveller.

'Where's Cap'en Armiger?'

Captain Borlinder pointed upwards, following the direction of his finger with one eye, as if that eye of faith could readily discern Rex among the angels.

'I thought he'd say that; I told you so, Lal, my dear. Keep your pluck up, and go tell Cap'en Holstius and Cap'en Wattles. They must hear the news too.'

'They here?'

Captain Borlinder changed colour. He had not thought of this possibility.

'In this very house, both of them,' replied the

Patriarch. 'Cap'en Wattles he's been backwards
and forwards between Liverpool and New York
and London all the time, with his business, and
Cap'en Holstius, he's just brought to port as fine
a cargo of white deal as you ever see. Yes,
they're both about.'

At this point they entered and shook
hands.

'And now,' continued the old man, 'let us
be comfortable. Keep your pecker up, Lal, my
dear, and give me a pipe. So I told you what he
would say, Lal. What a thing it is to have the
wisdom of fourscore! Now, my hearty, pay it
out.'

'I have set down on paper,' Captain Borlinder
began, 'a Narrative—ahem!—a Narrative of my
adventures since I started to find Cap'en Armiger.
If you please, I will read my Narrative.'

He lugged his precious manuscript out of his
pocket, unrolled it, coughed solemnly, and began
to read it.

'Stop,' interrupted the Patriarch; 'did you
try Moreton Bay?'

'No, I did not.'

Captain Zachariasen shook his head mournfully.

'Go on, my lad, go on,' he sighed; 'I doubt
it's no good.'

'Now, Venerable, keep your oar out,' said

Captain Borlinder, impatiently. 'You and your Moreton Bay! Lemme go on.'

He looked round him half ashamed of reading his own literary effort, spread the manuscript upon his knees, flattening it out, and smoothing down the dogs' ears. Then he began. He was, unfortunately, unacquainted with the rules of punctuation, so that his reading was hardly up to the Third Standard, the point at which, I believe, most school children stop. But the matter was clear and precise, so that the manner mattered little.

'I set sail,' he said, 'on January 3 from Southampton aboard the P. and O. steamer "Batavia," bound for Singapore, a second-class passenger.

'We navigated the Bay of Biscay, the weather being fine and the sea smooth. We had light showers and a breeze off Malta. We passed through the Canal and down the Red Sea—the weather being warm for the time of year, but cloudy, with much rain—to Aden. From Aden we sailed in a furious gale of wind to Point de Galle, and from Galle with a fair breeze and a smooth sea to Singapore, where we brought up all standing six weeks after leaving Southampton.

'At Singapore I began to look about me, making enquiries, but asking no questions for fear of arousing suspicion.'

'What suspicion?' asked Captain Zachariasen.

The reader hesitated. Then he read the passage over again.

'For fear of arousing suspicion.'

It was a phrase he had encountered somewhere or other in a somewhat limited course of reading, and he set it down, thinking that it sounded rather well.

'What suspicion?'

'If you don't keep your oar out,' he answered, 'we shall never get along.'

'What suspicion?' repeated Captain Zachariasen. 'Suspicion that you wanted to make away with the lad when you found him?'

'If you was five and forty years younger, my Patriarch,' returned the traveller, 'I'd let you know what suspicion. Now, Lal, if you'll believe me, my suspicion was that some one else beside me might tackle this job, and so spile it. I wanted it finished off workmanlike. So I cast about. Hold your old jaw, will you?'

He murmured something more in his throat which rumbled and echoed about the room like suppressed thunder.

'First, I went around the public-houses and hung about the bars.' Captain Zachariasen grunted. 'But nothing could I learn. Then I sat upon the wharf and went about the shipping. Mighty civil, well-spoken skippers they were, as a rule, but they could tell me nothing, though some of them knew the "Philippine," and one or two remembered Cap'en Armiger. It will be a comfort to you, Lal, to reflect that they all spoke well of him as a good sailor, who could carry his drink like a man.' Here Captain Zachariasen again grunted. 'So I saw what I had all along suspected, that I should have to go upon the search myself. First, therefore, I picked up such information as a man can come by as to the currents and the winds. This done, I laid down the supposed course of the boat, with such winds and such currents, on the chart. Now, you must know that Cap'en Armiger made a great mistake. So far from the current being N.E., and the wind S.W., the current sets in strong S.W. And the prevalent wind, less it's a monsoon or a cyclone, is S.W. too. What the devil are you grunting at now?' This is to Captain Zachariasen, who was making this sign again.

'Go on, my lad. Go on heavin'. Sooner we get to the bottom of the page the better.'

'Very well, then. Grunt and —— I beg your pardon, Lal. He's enough to make a bishop swear. Where was I? Oh! a cyclone, in S.W. too. What did I do then? Laid down on the map the place where that boat would likely make the land, and then I cast about to get a ship which would land me on that very identical spot. Sure

enough there was a boat in harbour just about to
sail.'

'What trade might she have been in?' asked
the Patriarch.

'Coal trade,' he replied, promptly. 'I took a
passage, bargained to be disembarked and called
for again in three weeks' time, and we set sail.
Beautiful sailing it is in those seas, and one of
these winter evenings, Lal, when you and me have
got nothing to do, I will tell you such yarns of
they islands as will make you long for to go there
yourself. Our course was south of Borneo, and
so into the narrow seas, through the Macassar
Straits, north of Celebes and Gillolo, and so along
the north-west of New Guinea, where I'd made up
my mind to find Cap'en Armiger. If you've got
a chart anywhere about, any of you, you might
follow.'

'Never mind the chart, my lad,' said Captain
Zachariasen ; 'go on.'

'Nobody, before me and Cap'en Armiger, had
ever landed on that desolate coast. They set me
ashore with six foot or so of baccy, a pipe, a box
of lucifers, a bottle of rum, a gun, and a small
fishing-net. That, I thought, would be enough to
carry me along for a spell, while I made my
enquiries.

'I found the natives black but friendly. They
appeared not to be cannibals. They greatly

admired my appearance and manners. They invited me to stay among them with the gun and be their king. And, although I was obliged to refuse, they were civil, and answered all my questions to the best of their capacities, which are naturally limited.'

Another grunt.

'After a bit I discovered that I had not been mistaken in my conclusions. Three years before, or thereabouts—because you cannot expect naked savages to be as accurate as us truth-telling Christians—a white man and a Malay had been washed ashore in an open boat.

'Directly I heard that I pricked up my ears. There might have been two different white men come ashore in an open boat, but not two pairs of white man and Malay man. That seemed impossible. So I up and enquired at once where they were.

'They told me that at landing there was a fight, but that they were taken up-country after the fight with their arms bound to their sides.' Here Captain Borlinder stopped. 'You remember, Venerable,' he said, 'how you interpreted that scrimmage shown by the dumb man? You were quite right.'

The Venerable grunted again.

'Of course,' the discoverer resumed, 'I made haste to find out which way they were taken, and it was not long before I started following their track, led by a native boy who knew the country well, having been born and brought up there.'

'Where were the rest of the natives born and brought up?' asked Captain Zachariasen. 'Go on, brother.   Reel it out.'

'The first day——' Captain Borlinder turned suddenly pale, as if a weak point had been discovered in his armour, and went on reading rapidly.   'The first day we made five-and-twenty miles, as near as I could reckon, going in a bee-line across country, over hills and valleys where lions, bears, tigers, hyænas, leopards, elephants, and hippopotamusses roamed free, seeking whom they may devour; cross rivers where crocodiles sat with open jaws snapping at the people as they passed by.'

'It is hot, I suppose, in these latitudes?' said Captain Zachariasen.

'Hottish,' replied the traveller.   'I was given to understand that it was their summer.   Hottish, walking.   Made a man relish his rum and water. And I found a pint of cold water with a jack-towel refreshing on a Saturday night.   The next day we made thirty knots of sandy desert, where there were camels and ostriches, and never a drop of water to make a cup of tea with.   The third day we crossed a mountain, twenty-five thousand feet high, on the sides of which were bears, wolves, and pemmican. From the summit we obtained a splendid view right across the China Seas, and with my glass I could easily make out Hong-Kong.

'On the fourth day, after doing thirty miles good, and living for a week on the bark of trees and wild roots, we passed through a thick forest inhabited solely by monkeys and snakes, after which we emerged upon a town, the like of which I had never expected to find in the heart of New Guinea. It appeared to consist of a million and a half of people, as near as I could learn. They go dressed in white cotton knee-breeches and turbans; they smoke cigarettes and drink Jamaica rum; their manners are pleasant and their ways hospitable.

'As soon as they saw that a white man had arrived, they flocked round me and began to ask questions. These I satisfied to the best of my power and requested to be taken to the king. They led me, or rather carried me, shouting along the streets, to the Royal Palace, which is a trifle bigger than the Crystal Palace, and all made of solid gold.

'The king is a young man, who wears his crown both day and night. He is always surrounded by his guards, and has to be approached on bended knees.

'After the usual compliments, he invited me to tell him what I came for.

'I replied that I was sent by the most beautiful girl in Rotherhithe—at this he seemed pleased, and said he wished she had come herself—in order to discover what had become of her sweetheart, named Rex Armiger, wrecked upon his majesty's coast in the year 1876.

'I confess that I felt sorry, when I had put the question, but then I had come all the way on purpose to put it. For the king and all his courtiers immediately burst into tears.

'I then learned the whole story.

'Cap'en Armiger had, in fact, landed on this shore, as I expected and calculated. He had been separated from his steward Dick in a scrimmage on the coast, and had been brought inland to be presented as a captive to the king. At the court he made himself at once a great favourite, being a good shot, which pleased his majesty, and a good dancer, which pleased the ladies. He lived three years with them in great favour with everybody, and at the end, though this you will hardly credit, engaged to be married to the king's sister, being by that time in despair of ever getting away.

'Unfortunately, only the week before I arrived, he was killed and devoured by a lion, and the princess was gone off her royal chump.

'I am truly sorry to be the bearer of such bad news, Lal. You will own that I done my best.

'The rest of my log, how I got away, and how I came here again, would not interest you now. You will, perhaps, like to hear them yarns in the long winter evenings when we have got nothing else to do.

' As for poor Cap'en Armiger, I brought away with me one relic of him—the last cap he ever wore. The king sent it to you by my hands. He said a great many civil things about my courage in coming all that way to find my friend, and I had to promise to go back again. However, that is nothing. Here, then, is Cap'en Armiger's cap —the cap of the Company.'

He untied the handkerchief and took out a cap with a gold band and a couple of anchors in silver embroidery upon the front. It was a uniform cap, that of the Indian Peninsular Company.

Lal received it, and turned it over in her hand, but with some doubt, stimulated by Captain Zachariasen's grunts.

The old man reached out his hand for the cap, examined it carefully, tried it on his own head, and grunted again.

'What are you grunting for now?' asked Captain Borlinder in great uneasiness.

'Gentlemen,' said Captain Zachariasen to the other two, 'tell me what you think?'

Captain Holstius made answer, like the country gentleman who read Gulliver's Travels, that he did not believe a word of it.   And why? Because no one who had read accounts of those latitudes could reconcile Captain Borlinder's Narrative with the tales of other travellers.

Captain Wattles shook his head.

'Coarse work,' he said. 'Very common, and coarse work.'

Upon this Captain Borlinder lost his temper, and behaved like an officer of his rank when in a rage upon his own quarter-deck.

'You shouldn't ha' thought, brother,' said the old man, holding out the cap and examining it with contempt, 'that a man of fourscore and odd could be taken in by such a clumsy jemmy as yourn.   I'd ha' spun a better yarn myself, by chalks.   Two things shall set you right.   First, my lad, this cap, which, I suppose, you bought on your way in Houndsditch, is the cap of a boy of thirteen, a midshipmite.   Now, Cap'en Armiger, like me, had a big head.   We may toss the cap into the fire, Lal, my pretty, because it isn't your sweetheart's cap, and never was.'   He did toss it into the fire, where it was immediately consumed, all except the gold lace which twisted into all shapes.   'Look at him!' he added.   'Sails in

gaily with a boy's cap in one hand and a yard and
half of lies, made up Lord knows where, in the
other. Another thing.' Captain Borlinder at
this juncture, because he had, in fact, bought that
cap in Houndsditch, presented every appearance
of discomfiture. 'When he landed among the
blacks, all alone, what language did he talk with
them? English? He knows no other. What
do you say, Cap'en Wattles?'

'Coarse work. Coarse and clumsy work.'

Captain Borlinder replied in general terms,
and endeavouring to bluster it out, that this was
hard for a man to bear, this was, after going
through all he had gone through.

But here Captain Wattles gave him the *coup
de grâce.*

'I can tell all of you where that precious
Narrative was written. For I made it my business to enquire at the London Docks. He has
been all the time aboard his own ship, and he
has made three voyages to Cadiz and back since
January. If you doubt, go and ask his people.'

This was an unexpected one. Captain Borlinder reeled.

Then Lal rose in her wrath.

'Go!' she cried. 'You are not fit to be
under the same roof with honest people. Go,
impudent liar! Oh, that men can be so wicked!
He has kept my Rex for six long months more in

his captivity. Go! let us never see your face again.'

She clenched her hands and pointed to the door with as threatening a gesture as Medea might have employed.

Captain Borlinder hastened to obey. He crammed the Narrative in his pocket, and his shiny hat upon his head, and walked forth, saying never a word. And although he has never since set foot upon the southern shores of the Port of London, I think he still sometimes feels over again the humiliation of that moment.

'And now,' said Captain Wattles, ' it is my turn. We have lost more than six months, it is true. I have settled all my business, and I have got command of a ship which trades among the islands, a Sydney schooner. I meant to tell you this to-day, not expecting to find this—this lying lubber here. Why, there ain't a lad of ten in the States that wouldn't put together a better story than that. Coarse and clumsy work.'

CHAPTER VIII.

THE QUEST OF CAPTAIN WATTLES.

THE next turn, therefore, fell to Captain Wattles. He, for his part, took leave in a quiet and business-like manner, making no protestations.

'I shall be,' he said, 'off and on about the Carolines, where we expect to find him. He is not in the regular track of the traders, else you would have heard from him. He is on none of the islands touched for pearl and *bêche de mer*— that we may be quite certain of; therefore, I shall try at those places which are seldom visited. If I find him, good; if not, I will let you know. I don't pretend to waste my time in looking for a man and nothing else; I am going to trade on my own account, and look about me the while. News runs from island to island in an astonishing way, and we shall likely hear about him. That's all I have to say, Miss Lal, and here's my hand upon it. Barnabas, the Son of Consolation, will act up to his name.' So he, too, disappeared.

Then, for a while, the house resumed its

usual aspect, and things went on as before. A letter came in due course from Captain Wattles. He had arrived at Sydney and was preparing for departure. Then no more letters.

The time passed slowly. Captain Holstius was away with his ship. The life and light seemed to have gone from the girl. Only the old man was left to cheer her continually, and Dick to raise her courage.

'I shall live, 'Lal, my dear,' he said, to see Cap'en Armiger come home again. I have no doubt of that; and, pretty, I've been thinking about the mummicker and the end of his story. Somehow, I doubt whether it wasn't him, and not the Cap'en, they took off to prison. I wish I could trust that Yankee chap; he's worse than the other. Now if the Norweegee could go——'

As for Barnabas, there was something in his cold and quiet way which impressed those who made his acquaintance. Such men, when they are on the right side, make good generals; when they are on the wrong, they provide the picturesque element of history. Thus in the sixteenth century he would have been invaluable as a buccaneer, being full of courage and as cool as a melon; also, under favourable conditions, he might have developed a fine religious fanaticism, under the influence of which he would have

hated a Spaniard and a Papist more than even
Sir Walter Raleigh hated him. In the seventeenth
century he would have found scope as a pirate,
with Madagascar, the West-Indian and Floridan
Keys, the harbours of Eastern Africa, and nearly
all the ports of South America for refuge; and
the navies of the world, with the rich galleons of
Spain, and the East-Indiamen of England for his
booty; and all the rogues and murderers afloat,
actual or possible, longing to become part of his
crew. In the eighteenth century the trade of
pirate fell into disrepute, by reason of the singu-
larly disagreeable end which happened to many
of its followers. Happily, that of privateer took
its place. In the present century, men like Barnabas B. Wattles have gone filibustering; have
carried black cargoes from the West Coast across
the Atlantic; and have gone blockade-running to
Charleston and Galveston. All these exciting
pursuits have come to an end; and there would
seem, at first sight, little for a sailor to find ready
for a willing hand to do, except perfectly legal
pursuits.

There is not much. Still, there is always
something. A man may carry Chinese coolies to
Trinidad, Peru, or Cuba. Under what pretences
he inveighs them aboard, what promises he makes
them, and how much he gets for each, no one,
outside the trade, which is a limited company,

knows or can discover. You might sooner hope
to learn the secrets of the Royal Arch. Again,
you may ship coolies for Réunion. They are
British subjects, but they are taken on board at
Pondicherry, which is a French settlement. And
the like mystery surrounds each transaction
in Hindoo flesh. Lastly, there is a delightful
pastime still carried on in Polynesia, known as the
Labour Traffic. Opinions differ as to the beneficial results of a few years of cooliedom in Queensland. For whereas some authorities say that the
Polynesian learns the blessings of second-hand
reach-me-downs, with a smattering of Christianity,
with which to astonish his relatives, the Browns,
on his return ; others declare that the extra gar-
ments are discarded as soon as he lands, the
rudiments of the Christian faith forgotten, and
only the taste for rum remains. I know not
which is right, because in order to decide the
point, one ought to live along with native Polynesians, or with Australian colonists, in order to
hear both sides of the question, and no contro-
versialist has as yet done that. One thing, however, is quite certain, that the coolies embark for
various reasons, among which no one has as yet
pretended to find a desire to toil on the Queensland cotton and sugar estates. Toil of any kind
is, indeed, the last thing which these children of
the Equatorial Pacific desire. Rest is what they

love, or, if any exercise, then a languid swim in tepid waters, a dance in the evening, and the joyous cup. Now to ship these innocents and to bring them to the market where they may be hired is a profitable, albeit a dangerous, pursuit.

It is never a fault of the American adventurer that he too carefully considers the danger. Where there are dollars to be picked up there is generally danger. The round earth may be mapped out in different belts of fertility, so far as dollars are concerned. Where they most abound and may most readily be gathered there is such a crowd, with so much fighting and struggling, or there are so many perils from climate, crocodiles, settlers, snakes, natives, and sharks, that it is only the brave man who ventures thither, and only the strong man who comes home in safety, bringing with him the treasures he has fought for. Barnabas B. Wattles was brave and strong, and he knew the islands of old, where he had sojourned, though certainly not, as we have once heard him state, as a missionary. He now saw his way to a neat stroke of business combined with love. He would prove, not clumsily, as did his rival, but prove beyond a doubt, the death of Rex Armiger. Then he would return, carry off the girl with the money, which he supposed belonged to her, forgetting the existence of Mrs. Rydquist, and get

back to America, where he knew of a certain
dry dock, to possess which was the dream of his
soul. It may be also stated that he firmly believed that the man was dead, and to find Rex
Armiger alive was the last thing which he expected.

Yet this, as you will see, was exactly what he
did find.

He took command of his trading schooner,
loaded her with the things which Polynesians
love, such as gaudy cottons, powder, tobacco,
rum, and strong perfumes, and set sail.

It is not my purpose to follow the voyage of
the ' Fair Maria ' across the Pacific Ocean, nor to
tell of the various adventures which befell her
captain, and the trade he did. Wherever he
touched he made enquiries, but he could hear
nothing of a young white man cast ashore in an
open boat. No one knew or had heard of any
such jetsam.

At last he began to think his search would
lead to nothing, and that all trace of the man was
lost. This he regretted, because he was un-
feignedly anxious to send home or bring home
proofs of his death ; so anxious that he had grown
perfectly certain that Rex was dead.

It came to pass, however, after many days
that he sighted an island, an outlying member of
a group at which he knew that traders never

touch, because it was too small a place and lay out of the usual track.

It is very well known that a large number of the Caroline Islands are composed of certain coral formations called atolls. These consist of a round ring of rock just appearing above the surface, enclosing a shallow lagoon, whose diameter varies from a few yards to a hundred miles, in which lie islands, some of them large islands with hills, streams, and splendid woods of cocoa-palm, bread-fruit, durian, and pandang ; whose islanders lead, or would lead if they knew how, delightful lives in fishing in their smooth waters, eating the fruits which Heaven sends, and doing no kind of work. Others there are, small atolls with small lagoons, whose islets are mere rocks on which grow nothing but the universal pandang, the screw palm, which serves the people for everything. Such was this. It was too insignificant even to have a name ; it was distant about two hundred miles from the group of which it might be supposed to be a member ; it was simply laid down on the chart as a ‘shoal,’ and had, perhaps, never been visited by any ship since its first discovery.

Moved by some impulse, perhaps, a mere curiosity as to the capabilities of trade and the possibility of pearls, Captain Wattles steered towards this low-lying land.

When his boat lay upon the shallow waters

within the reef he found a group of the inhabitants of the principal islet gathered upon the beach.   They were of the brown Polynesian race, and were apparently preparing for a hostile reception.

Among them stood, passive, a man almost as brown as themselves, but with fair hair and blue eyes.   He was a white man; he was a young white man; he was evidently no common beachcomber; and Captain Wattles immediately recognised, without any doubt, the man of whom he was in search.   He was dressed in rags; the sleeves were torn from his jacket and his bare arms were tattooed; his trousers had lost most of their legs; he wore some kind of sandals made of the pandang leaf; his beard was long, his hair was hanging in an unkempt mass; his head was protected from the sun by an ingenious arrangement of another leaf of the same tree.   It could be no other than Rex Armiger.

A strange feeling, akin to pity, seized on Captain Wattles.   He repressed it, as unworthy of himself.   But he did at first feel pity for him.

The white man stood among the natives afraid to excite their suspicion by running before them to meet the boat: yet his eagerness was visible in his attitude, in the trembling of his lips, in the way in which he looked upon the boat.

He carried a short lance in his hand like all the rest.

Captain Wattles rowed within hailing distance of the shore.   Then he stood up.

'White man, ahoy ! '

The white man said something to his companions, and stepped forward, but in a leisurely manner, as if he was not at all anxious to speak the boat.

He came to the water's edge and sat down.

'I am an Englishman,' he said, speaking slowly, because he was speaking a language he had not used for three years. 'I am an Englishman. My name is Armiger. I was the captain of the Indian Peninsular ship " Philippine," wrecked on a shoal three years or so ago. I have been living since among these people.'

'Do you know their lingo ? '

'Yes.'

'Then tell them I am harmless and I want to row nearer land.'

Rex turned to the men and addressed them in their own language.

They all sat down and waited.

'You may come nearer,' he said ; 'but make no movement that may alarm them, and do not attempt to land. They are suspicious since two years ago a ship came down from the Ladrone

Islands and kidnapped twenty of them, including a Malay, cast away with me.'

Here then was the interpretation of Dick's second pantomimic fight. He did not escape, he was kidnapped. How he got away from the Ladrone Islands, how he found his way to England, remains a matter hitherto undiscovered.

Captain Wattles brought up his boat within a few yards of the beach, but in deep water, holding his men in readiness to give way.

Sitting in the stern he was able to talk freely with Rex, who stood at the very edge of the water waiting for an opportunity to leap on board.

' So,' said Captain Wattles, ' you are Cap'en Armiger, are you ?'

Rex was astonished at the salutation.

' Why ? Do you know me?'

' You see I know your name, stranger. I confess I am sorry to find you. I thought you were dead. I hardly calculated that I'd find you, though I certainly did promise to keep one eye open for you.'

' What promise ? ' asked Rex.

' I promised—— We'll come to that directly. Now, what are those black devils dancing about for ?'

The natives had jumped to their feet, and were now shaking clubs and spears in a threatening way.

'They want my assurance,' Rex said, 'that you are not a black-birder.'

'Honest trading schooner,' replied Captain Wattles. 'Tell them they may come aboard and see for themselves. What have they got to sell?'

'What should we have on this little island? We live on kabobo. Do you want to buy any? What is your name?'

'Barnabas B. Wattles, cap'en of the "Fair Maria," lying yonder. Guess you'd like to be aboard her. Well, business first. Let's trade something. Got no turtle?'

'No.'

'No *bêche de mer*? No copra?'

'We have nothing.'

'Very well, then,' said Captain Wattles. 'After business, pleasure. Mate, I guess you are tired of this gem of the sea—eh?'

'So tired,' replied Rex Armiger, 'that if you had not turned up I believe I should have made a raft out of the pandang leaves and tried my luck.'

'Then I'm devilish glad we came,' said Captain Wattles. 'The more so as I have a little bargain to propose before you come aboard my craft.'

'Any bargain that's fair.'

'I guess this is quite fair and honourable,' the Captain went on. 'You have been a beach-comber upon this island for nigh upon three years. Three years is a long time. The gell you were in

love with has likely got tired of waiting. Your
name is wrote off the books ; your ship is long
since posted ; your friends have put on mourning
for you——'

. ' What's the good of so much talk?' interrupted
Rex. 'I want to be taken off this island. What's
your bargain?'

'Fair and easy, lad. Let me have my talk
out.' Captain Wattles looked at him with a
curious expression. 'Why, you are as good as
dead already.'

' What do you mean?'

' I mean this. There's one or two men who
would like you to be dead. I'm one of those.
What's more, I ain't goin', for my part, to be the
means of restoring you to life. No, sir. I don't
exactly wish you dead, and yet I don't want to
see you alive in England.'

This was said with great decision.

Rex listened with amazement.

' What harm have I ever done to you, man?'
he cried. ' You wish me dead?'

' There's no use keeping secrets between us two,'
continued the strange trader. ' Look here, three
years ago, before you got command of the
" Philippine," you were in love with a certain
young lady who lives at Rotherhithe.'

' Go on. For God's sake, go on.'

' That sweet young thing, sir, whom it's a

privilege to know and a pride to fall in love with, peaked and pined more than a bit, thinkin' about you and wonderin' where you were.'

'Poor Lal! dear Lal!'

'Yes, she was real faithful and kindhearted, that gell. Her friends, and especially her mother, who takes a kind of pleasure in reckoning up the dead men she knows located at the bottom of the briny, gave you up. But she never gave you up. No, never.'

'Poor Lal! dear Lal!'

The tears stood in the castaway's eyes as he sat and listened. Behind him the men of the island stood like wild beasts on the alert, waiting for the moment of flight or attack. And also like wild beasts, they were never certain whether to fly or to fight.

'No one like that gell, sir, no one,' continued Captain Wattles; 'which is all the more reason why other fellows want to cut in.'

Rex began to understand.

'Among other fellows is myself, Barnabas B. Wattles. Very good. Now you see why I would rather hear that you were dead than alive, and why I'm darned disappointed to meet you here. However, you are on about as desolate a place as I know of, that's one comfort.'

The fact brought no comfort to Rex, but quite the reverse.

'Mate, I want to tell you the whole story fair and above board. I will tell you no lies. Therefore, you may trust what I say. And first let me know how you came here, and all about it.'

Rex told his story. It was all as Lal had divined from Dick's action. They sighted the island, being then half dead with hunger, and with difficulty managed to paddle themselves ashore. They were seized by the natives, and a consultation was held whether they should be killed. They were spared.

Life on that island is necessarily simple. The people live entirely on kabobo, which is a sort of rough bread made of the pandang nut. They have no choice, because there is nothing else to live upon. It is the only tree that grows upon this lonely land. Kabobo is said to be wholesome, but it is monotonous.

Rex explained briefly that he had learned to talk with them, and won by slow degrees their confidence ; that he had taught them a few simple things, and he was regarded by them with some sort of affection ; that, after a year's residence on the island, a ship came in sight, but did not anchor. That a boat put off, manned by an armed crew, who, when the people came down to meet them, half disposed to be friendly, attacked them, killed some, and carried off others, among whom was the Malay. This made them extremely suspicious.

Since that event nothing had happened; nothing but the slow surge of the wave upon the reef and the sigh of the wind in the pandang trees.

'Now that you have come,' Rex concluded,. 'you who know—her,' he added cheerfully, though his heart was heavy in thinking of the bargain, 'you will take me off this island—for her sake.'

'For her sake?' echoed Captain Wattles. 'Man alive! It is for her sake that I won't do no such silly thing. No, sir. You understand that she thinks you're alive. Very good then. Bein' a faithful gell, she keeps her word with you. Once she knows you are dead, why, there will be a chance for another chap. And who so likely as the man who came all the way out here to discover that interestin' fact? See, pard?'

'Good God!' cried Rex. 'Do you mean that you will leave me here and say I am dead?'

'That is exactly what I am coming to, Cap'en Armiger. I take it, sir, that you air a sensible man, and I have been told that you know better than most which way that head of yours is screwed on. You can understand what it is to be in love with that most beautiful creature. What you've got to do is to buy your freedom.'

'How am I to buy my freedom?'

'I've thought of this meeting, sir.'—this was a happy invention of the moment—'and I considered within myself what would be best. The easiest way out of it, the way most men would choose, would be to get up a little shindy with those brown devils there and to take that opportunity of dropping a bead into your vitals. That way, I confess, did seem to me, at first sight, the best. By why kill a man when you needn't? I know it's foolish, but I should like to go back to that young creature without thinking that she'd disapprove if she knew.'

Rex sprang to his feet. The man who lay there in the stern of the boat, six feet from the shore, his head upon his hands, calmly explaining why he did not murder him, was going back to England to marry Lal—his Lal. To marry her! He threw up his arms and was speechless with rage and horror.

Behind him the savages stood grouped, waiting for any sign from him to fly or rush upon the strangers with their spears.

The day was perfectly calm, the sea was motionless in the land-locked water, and, in the calm and peace of the hot noonday, the words fell upon his brain like words one hears in a ghastly dream of the night.

' Yes,' the man went on, ' I want to do what is right, and this is my proposal, Cap'en Armiger. I know you can be trusted, because I've made enquiries. Some Englishmen can lie like Rooshans, but some can't. You, I am told, are one of that sort who can't. Promise me to drop your own name, not to go back to England for twenty years at least, never to let out that you are Rex Armiger, to stay in these seas, and I'll take you aboard my schooner and land you at Levuka or Honolulu, or wherever you please. Come, you may even go to Australia if you like. As for names, I'll lend you mine. You shall have the name of my brother, Jacob B. Wattles, now in Abraham's bosom. He won't mind, and if he does, it don't matter. As for work, there's plenty to get and plenty to do among these islands. There's the labour traffic; there's pearl-fishing; there's trading. You may live among them, marry among them, turn beach-comber for life; you may get to Fiji and run a plantation. Cap'en Armiger, if I were you, I would rather not go back.

'As for this place, now, I don't suppose a man grows to get a yearning for kabobo for a permanence, and on this darned one-horse island there doesn't seem much choice outside the pandang tree. Likewise, those young gentlemen with their toothpicks are not quite the company you were brought up to, I reckon. Whereas, except for the missionaries, who spoil everything, I don't suppose there's better company to be got anywhere in this world than you'll find in this ocean when I land you on an island worth the name. At Honolulu, for instance, there's nobblers and champagne, and—— Wal, I'd rather live there, or in one or two other islands that I know, than anywhere in Europe or the States. And so would you, come to look at things rightly.'

Rex still kept silence, pacing on the narrow beach.

'As for being dead, you've been dead for three years, so that can't be any objection. Why, man, I give you life; I resurrect you. Think' of that!

'As for being altered, you are so changed that your own mother would not know you again. No fear of any old friends recognising you. And, so far as a few dollars go to start with, say the word and you shall have them, with a new rig-out.'

Still Rex made no reply.

'There is my offer, plain and open. I'm sorry for you, Cap'en Armiger, I re'lly am, because she's out an' out the best set-up gell that walks. But two men can't both have her. And I mean to be the man that does—not you. And all is fair in love.'

'And if I refuse your offer?'

'Then, Cap'en Armiger, you stay just where you now happen to be. And a most oncomfortable location. Now, sir, make no error. Since the day that you landed on this island, have you seen ary a sail on the sea? No. Ships don't come here. Even the Germans at Yap know that it's no manner of good coming here. You are out of the reach of hurricanes, so you can't expect so much as a wreck. You are hundreds of miles from any land; you have got no tools to make a raft, and no provisions to put aboard her if you could make one; you are altogether lonely, and hopeless, and destitute. Robinson Crusoe hadn't a more miserable a look-out. As for that young lady, you have no chance, not the least mite of a chance, sir, of seeing her ever again. You have lost her. Why, then, give her another chance, and let me say you are dead. Cap'en, you can write—that's another of my conditions— a last dying will and testament on a bit o' paper, which I will send her. Come, be reasonable.'

Rex stood still, staring blankly before him. On the one hand, liberty and life—for to stay upon the island was death; on the other, perhaps a hopeless prison.

Yet—Lal Rydquist! If she mourned him as one dead, would it hurt to let her mourn until she forgot him? He shuddered as he thought of her marrying the cold-blooded villain before him. Perhaps she would never marry anyone, but go on in sadness all her days.

I am happy to say that the third course open to him—to give his parole and then to break it —did not occur to him as possible.

He decided according to the nobler way.

'Go without me,' he said. And then, without a word of reproach or further entreaty, he left the beach and walked away, and was lost among the palm-trees standing thickly upon the thin and sandy soil.

Captain Wattles gazed after him in admiration.

'There goes,' he said, 'one of the real old sort. Bully for the British bulldog yet!'

The group of savages stood still, looking on and wondering. They suspected many things: that their white prisoner would run away with the boat; that the crew might fire upon them or try to kidnap them. They also hoped a few things, such as that the white captain would give them things, fine beads, fine coloured stuffs, or rum to get drunk with. Yet nothing happened. Then Captain Wattles, seeing that Rex Armiger had disappeared, bethought him of something. And he began to make signs to the black fellows and to show them from the stern of his boat things wonderful and greatly to be desired, and at the same time he gave certain directions to his crew.

Thereupon the savages, moved with the envy

and desire of those things, did with one accord advance a few yards nearer.

Captain Wattles spread out more things, holding them up in the sun for their admiration, and making signs of invitation.

They then divided into two groups, of whom one retreated and the other advanced.

Captain Wattles next displayed a couple of most beautiful knives, the blades of which, when he opened them, flashed in the sun in a most surprising manner. And he pointed to two of the islanders, young and stalwart fellows, and invited them by gestures to come into the water and take these knives.

The crew meantime remained perfectly motionless, hands on oars. Only those experienced in rowing might have observed that their oars were well forward ready for the stroke.

The advanced group again separated into two more groups, of which one consisting of a dozen of the younger men, including the two invited, advanced still nearer, until they were close to the water's edge, and the others retreated further back. All of them, both those behind and those in front, remained watchful and suspicious, like a herd of deer.

Presently the two singled out plunged into the water and swam out to the boat. At first they swam round it, while Captain Wattles continued to smile pleasantly at them and to exhibit the knives. Also the crew dipped their oars without the least noise, and with a half stroke, short and sharp, not moving their bodies, got a little way upon the boat. The swimmers, with their eyes upon the knives, did not seem to notice this manœuvre. Nor did they suspect though the oars were dipped again and the boat fairly moving.

For just then they made up their minds that Captain Wattles was a kind and benevolent person, and they swam close to the stern of the vessel and held up their hands for the knives.

It is very well known that the Polynesian natives have long and thick black hair, which they tie up in a knot at the top of their heads.

What, then, was the surprise of these two poor fellows to find their top-knots grasped, one by Captain Wattles, and the other by his interpreter, and their own heads held under water till they were half drowned, while the crew gave way and the boat shot out to sea.

There was a wild yell of the natives on shore, and a rush to the water. But the boat was too far out for missiles to reach or shouts to terrify.

'Now,' said Captain Wattles, when the half-drowned fellows were hauled up the ship's side,

' we didn't exactly want this kind o' cargo, and I had hoped to have stuck to legitimate trade. Wal! this will make it very awkward for the next ship which touches here, and I don't think it will add to Captain Armiger's popularity. After all,' he added, ' I doubt I was a fool not to finish this job and have done with it. Who knows but some blundering ship may find out the place by mistake and pick him up?'

When the ' Fair Maria ' returned to Sydney, some months later, the very first thing Captain Wattles did was .to put into the post a bulky letter.

Like Captain Borlinder he had written a Narrative. Unlike that worthy's story, this had all the outward appearance of *vraisemblance*. I would fain enrich this history with it, at length, but forbear. Yet it was a production of remarkable merit, combining so much that was true with so much that was false.

As a basis we may recall the history, briefly touched upon, of the kidnapping by the ship from the Ladrones.

This story put Captain Wattles upon the track of as good a tale of adventure, ending with the death of Rex Armiger, as was ever told. Some day, perhaps, with changed names, it may see the light as a tale for boys.

The local colouring was excellent, and the

writer's knowledge of the natives made every detail absolutely correct. It ended by an appeal, earnest, religious, to Lal's duties as a Christian. No woman, said Captain Barnabas, was allowed to mourn beyond a term ; nor was any woman (by the Levitical law) allowed to consider herself as belonging to one man, should that man die. Wherefore, he taught her, it was her bounden duty to accept the past as a thing to be put away and done with.

'We forget,' he concluded, 'the sorrows of childhood; the hopes and disappointments of early youth are remembered no more by healthy minds. So let it be with the memory of the brave and good man who loved you, doubtless faithfully as you loved him. Do not hide it, or stifle it. Let it die away into a recollection of sadness endured with resignation. I would to Heaven that it had been my lot to touch upon this island, where he lived so long, before the fatal event which carried him off. I would that it had been my privilege to bring him home with me to your arms. I cannot do this now. But when I return to England, and call at Seven Houses, may it be my happiness to administer that consolation which becomes one who bears my christian-name.'

This was very sweet and beautiful. Indeed, Captain Wattles had a poetical spirit, and would doubtless have written most sweet verses had he turned his attention to that trade.

After the letter was posted, he was sitting in a verandah, his feet up, reading the latest San Francisco paper. Suddenly he dropped it, and turned white with some sudden shock.

His friends thought he would faint, and made haste with a nobbler which he drank. Then he sat up in his chair and said solemnly:

'I have lost the sweetest gell in all the world, through the darndest folly! Don't let any man ask me what it was. I had the game in my own hands, and I threw it away. Mates! I sha'n't never—no, never—be able to hold my head up again. A nobbler? Ten nobblers!'

The letter reached England in due course, and, for reasons which will immediately appear, was opened by Captain Zachariasen. He read it aloud right through twice. Then he put it down, and the skin of his face wrinkled itself in a thousand additional crow's-feet, and a ray of profound wisdom beamed from his sagacious eyes, and he said slowly:

'Mrs. Rydquist, ma'am, I said at first go off that I didn't trust that Yankee any more than the Borlinder lubber. Blame me if they ain't both in the same tale. You and me, ma'am, will live to see!'

'I hope we may, Captain Zachariasen ; I hope we may.   Last night I lay awake three hours, and I heard voices.   We have yet to learn what these voices mean.   Winding-sheets in candles I never knew to fail, but voices are uncertain.'

CHAPTER IX.

THE GREAT GOOD LUCK OF CAPTAIN HOLSTIUS.

THE clumsy cheat of Captain Borlinder brought home to Lal the sad truth that nobody, except herself and perhaps Captain Holstius, believed Rex could still be living. Even the Doctor of the 'Aryan,' who called every time the ship came home, frankly told her that he could not think it possible for him to be anywhere near the track of ships without being heard of. The Company had sent to every port touched by Pacific traders, and to every missionary station, asking that enquiry should be made, but nothing had been heard. All the world had given him up. There came a time when anxiety became intolerable, with results to nerve and brain which might have been expected had Lal's friends possessed any acquaintance with the diseases of the imagination.

'I must do something,' she said one day to Captain Holstius, who remonstrated with her for doing too much. 'I must be working; I cannot sit still. All day I think of Rex—all night I see

Rex—waiting on the shore of some far-off land, looking at me with reproachful eyes, which ask why I do not send someone to take him away. In my dreams I try to make him understand— alas! he will not hear me, and only shakes his head when I tell him that one man is looking for him now, and another will follow after.'

Captain Holstius, slowly coming to the conclusion that the girl was falling into a low condition, began to cast about, in his thoughtful way, for a remedy. He took a voyage to Norway to think about it.

Very much to Lal's astonishment, he reappeared a month later, without his ship. He told her, looking a little ashamed of himself, that he had come by steamer, and that he had made a little plan which, with her permission, he would unfold to her.

'I drew the shortest straw,' he said; 'otherwise I should have gone long ago. Now, without waiting for Captain Wattles, who may be an honest man or he may not be —— '

'Not be,' echoed the Patriarch.

'I mean to go at once.'

Lal clasped her hands.

'But there is another thing,' he went on. 'Lal, my dear, it isn't good for you to sit here waiting; it isn't good for you to be looking upon that image all day long as well as all night.'

'It never leaves me now,' she cried, the tears in her eyes. 'Why, I see him now, as I see him always while you are talking—while we are all sitting here.'

Indeed, to the girl's eyes, the figure stood out clear and distinct.

'See!' she said, 'a low beach with palm-trees, such as you read to me about last year. He is on the sands, gazing out to sea. His eyes meet mine. Oh, Rex—Rex! how can I help you? What can I do for you?'

Captain Holstius shuddered. It seemed as if he, too, saw this vision.

Captain Zachariasen said that mummicking was apt to spread in a family like measles.

'Then, Lal dear,' said Captain Holstius, 'hear my plan. I have sold my share in the ship. I got a good price for it—three hundred pounds. I am ready to start to-morrow. But I fear that when I am gone you will sit here and grieve worse because I shall not be here to comfort you. It is the waiting that is bad. So'—he hesitated here, but his blue eyes met Lal's with an honest and loyal look—'so, my dear, you must trust yourself to me, and we will go together and look for him.'

'Go with you?'

'Yes; go with me. With my three hundred pounds we can get put from port to port, or pay the captain of a trader to sail among the Carolines with us on board. I daresay it will be rough, but ship captains of all kinds are men to be trusted, you know, and I shall be with you. You will call me your brother, and I shall call you my sister, if you like.'

To go with him! Actually to sail away across the sea in quest of her lover! To feel that the distance between them was daily growing less! This seemed at first sight an impossible thing, more unreal than the vision of poor Rex.

To be sure such a plan would not be settled in a day. It was necessary to get permission from Mrs. Rydquist, whose imagination would not at first rise to the Platonic height of a supposed brotherhood.

She began by saying that it was an insult to the memory of her husband, and that a daughter of hers should go off in broad daylight was not what she had expected or hoped. She also said that if Lal was like other girls she would long since have gone into decent crapes and shown resignation to the will of Heaven. That fair warning with unmistakable signs had been given her; that, after all, she was no worse off than her mother; with more to the same effect. Finally, if Lal chose to go away on a wild goose chase, she would not, for her part, throw any obstacle in the way, but she supposed that her daughter intended to marry Captain Holstius whether she picked up Rex or not.

' He ought, my dear,' said Captain Zachariasen, meaning the Norweegee, ' to have been a naval chaplain, such is his goodness of heart. And as gentle as a lamb, and of such are the kingdom of heaven. You may trust yourself to him as it were unto a bishop's apron. And if 'twill do you any good, my pretty, to sail the salt seas o'er in search of him, who may be for aught we know, but we hope he isn't, lying snug at the bottom, why take and up and go. As for the Captains, I'll keep 'em in order, and with authority to give a month's warning, I'll sit in the kitchen every morning and keep 'em at it. Your mother can go on goin' on just the same with her teapot and her clean handkerchiefs.'

This was very good of the old man, and in the end he showed himself equal to the task, so that Rydquist's fell off but little in reputation while Lal was away.

As for what people might say, it was very well known in Rotherhithe who and of what sort was Lal Rydquist, and why she was going away. If unkind things were spoken, those who spoke them might go to regions of ill repute, said the Captains in discussion.

How the good fellows passed round the hat to buy Lal a kit complete; how Captain Zachariasen discovered that he had a whole bag full of golden sovereigns which he did not want, and would never want; how it was unanimously resolved that Dick must go with them; how the officers of the 'Aryan' for their share provided the passage-money to San Francisco and back for this poor fellow; how the Director of the Company, who had come with the Secretary to see the 'mummicking,' heard of it, and sneaked to Rotherhithe unknown to anybody with a purse full of bank-notes and a word of good wishes for the girl; how everybody grew amazingly kind and thoughtful, not allowing Lal to be put upon or worried, so that servants did what they ought to do without being looked after, and meals went on being served at proper times, and the Captains left off bringing things that wanted buttons; how Mrs. Rydquist for the first time in her life received supernatural signs of encouragement; and how they went on board at last, accompanied by all the Captains—these things belong to the great volumes of the things unwritten.

All was done at last, and they were in the Channel steaming against a head wind and a chopping sea. They were second-class passengers, of course; money must not be wasted. But what mattered rough accommodation?

All the way across to New York on the 'Rolling Forties' they had head winds and rough seas.

Yet what mattered bad weather? It began with a gale from the south-west in the Irish Sea, which bucketed the ship about all the way from the Mersey to Queenstown. The sailors stamped about the deck all night, and there was a never-ending yo-ho-ing with the dashing and splashing of the waves over the deck. The engines groaned aloud at the work they were called upon to do; the ship rolled and pitched without ceasing; the passengers were mostly groaning in their cabins, and those who could get out could get no fresh air except on the companion, for it was impossible to go on deck; everything was cold, wet, and uncomfortable. Yet there was one glad heart on board who minded nothing of the weather. It was the heart of the girl who was going in quest of her lover; so that every moment brought them nearer to him, what mattered for rough weather? Besides, Lal was not sea-sick, nor was her companion, as by profession forbidden that weakness.

When they left Queenstown the gale, which had been south-west, became north-west, which was rather worse for them, because it was colder. And this gale was kept up for their benefit the whole way across, so that they had no easy moment, nor did the ship once cease her plunging through angry waters, nor did the sun shine upon them at all, nor did the fiddles leave the tables, nor were the decks dry for a moment. Yet what mattered wind and rain and foul weather? For every moment brought the girl nearer to her lost lover.

When Lal stood on the rolling deck, clinging to the arm of Captain Holstius, and looked across the grey waters leaden and dull beneath the cloudy sky, it was with a joy in her heart which lent them sunshine.

'I see Rex no longer in my dreams,' she said; 'what does that man?'

'It means, Lal,' replied Captain Holstius, who believed profoundly that the vision was sent direct by Providence, 'that he is satisfied, because he knows that you are coming.'

Some of the passengers perceiving that here was an extremely pretty girl, accompanied by a brother—brothers are not generally loth to transfer their sisters to the care of those who can appreciate them more highly—endeavoured to make acquaintance, but in vain. It was not in order to talk with young fellows that Lal was crossing the ocean.

Then, the voyage having passed through like a dream, they landed at New York, and another dream began in the long journey across the continent among people whose ways and speech were strange.

This is a journey made over land, and there was no more endurance other than that of patience.

But it is a long and tedious journey which even the ordinary traveller finds weary, while to Lal, longing to begin the voyage of search, it was well-nigh intolerable. Some of the passengers began to remark this beautiful girl with eyes that looked always westward as the train ploughed on its westward way. She spoke little with her companion, who was not her husband and did not seem to be her brother. But from time to time he unrolled a chart for her, and they followed a route upon the ocean, talking in undertones. Then these passengers became curious, and one or two of them, ladies, broke through the American reserve towards strangers and spoke to the English girl, and discovered that she was a girl with a story of surpassing interest. She made friends with these ladies, and after a while she told them her story, and how the man with whom she travelled was not her brother at all, and not even her cousin, but her very true and faithful friend, her lover, more loyal than Amadis de Gaul, who had sold all that he had and brought the money to her that she might go herself to seek her sweetheart. And then she told what reason she had to believe that Rex was living, and pointed to the Malay who had brought the message from the sea, and was as faithful to her as any bull-dog.

They pressed her hands and kissed her; they wished her God-speed upon her errand, and they wondered what hero this lover of hers could be, since, for his sake, she could accept without offer of reward the service, the work, the very fortune of so good and unselfish a man.

He was no hero, in truth, poor Rex! nor was he, I think, so good a man as Captain Holstius; but he was her sweetheart, and she had given him her word.

Yet, although she talked, although the journey was shortened by the sympathy of these kind friends, it was like the voyage, a strange and unreal dream; it was a dream to be standing in the sunshine of California; a dream to look upon the broad Pacific; a dream that her brother stood beside her with thoughtful eyes and parted lips, looking across the ocean on which their quest was to be made.

' Yes, Lal,' he murmured, pointing where westward lie the lands we call Far East, ' yonder, over the water, are the Coral Islands. They are scattered across the sea for thousands of miles, and on one of them sits Captain Armiger. Doubt not, my dear, that we shall find him.'

Now it came to pass that the thing for which a certain English girl, accompanied by a Norwegian sea-captain, had come to San Francisco became noised abroad in the city, and even got into the papers, and interviewers called upon Captain Holstius begging for particulars, which he supplied, saying nought of his own sacrifices, nor of the money, and how it was obtained.

The story, dressed up in newspaper fashion, made a very pretty column of news. It was copied, with fresh dressing up, into the New York papers, and accounts of it, with many additional details, all highly dramatic, were transmitted by the various New York correspondents—all of whom are eminent novelists—to the London papers. The story was copied from them by all the country and colonial papers, whence it came that the story of Lal's voyage, and the reason of it became known, in garbled form, all over the English-speaking world. But, as a great quantity of most interesting and exciting things, including the Irish discussion, have happened during this year, public interest in the voyage was not sustained, and it was presently forgotten, and nobody enquired into the sequel.

This, indeed, is the fate of most interesting stories as told by the papers. An excellent opening leads to nothing.

But the report of her doings was of great service to Lal in San Francisco. In this wise. Among those who came to see the beautiful English girl in search of her sweetheart was a lady with whom she had travelled from New York, and to whom she had told her story. This lady brought her husband. He was a rich man

just then, although he had recently spent a winter
and spring in Europe. A financial operation,
which was to have been a Bonanza boom, has
since then smashed him up; but he is beginning
again in excellent heart, none the worse for the
check, and is so generous a man that he deserves
to make another pile. He is, besides, so full of
courage, resource, quickness, and ingenuity that
he is quite certain to make it. Also, he is so
extravagant that he will most assuredly lose it
again.

'Miss Rydquist,' He said, 'my wife has told
me your story. Believe me, young lady, you
have everybody's profound sympathy, and I am
here, not out of curiosity, because I am not
a press man, but to tell you that perhaps I
can be of some help to you if you will let
me.'

'My dear,' said his wife, interrupting, 'we do
not know yet whether you will let us help you,
and we are rather afraid of offering. May we
ask whether—whether you are sure you are rich
enough for what may turn out a long and expensive voyage?'

'Indeed,' said Lal, 'I do not know. Captain
Holstius sold his share in a ship, and that brought
in a good deal of money, and other friends helped
us, and I think we have about five hundred
pounds left.'

'That is a good sum to begin with,' said the American. 'Now, young lady, is your—your brother what is reckoned a smart sailor?'

'Oh yes.' Lal was quite sure about this. 'Everybody in the Commercial Docks always said he was one of the best seamen afloat.'

'So I should think. Now then. A week or two ago—so that it seems providential—I had to take over a trading schooner as she stands, cargo and all. She's in the bay, and you can look at her. But—she has no skipper.'

'Now,' said his wife, 'you see how we might help you, my dear. My husband does not care where his ship is taken to, nor where she trades. If it had not been for this accident of your arrival, he would have sold her. If Captain Holstius pleases, he can take the command, and sail wherever he pleases.'

This was a piece of most astonishing good fortune, because it made them perfectly independent. And, on the other hand, it was not quite like accepting a benefit and giving nothing in return, because there was the trading which might be done.

In the end, there was little profit from this source, as will be seen.

Therefore they accepted the offer with grateful hearts.

A few days later they were sailing across the

blue waters in a ship well manned, well found, and seaworthy. With them was a mate who was able to interpret.

Then began the time which will for ever seem to Lal the longest and yet the shortest in her life, for every morning she sighed and said, ' Would that the evening were here !' and every evening she longed for the next morning. The days were tedious and the nights were long. Now that they are all over, and a memory of the past, she recalls them, one by one, each with its little tiny incident to mark and separate it from the rest, and remembers all, with every hour, saying, ' This was the fortieth day before we found him,' and ' Thirty days after this day we came to the island of my Rex.'

The voyage, after two or three days of breeze, was across a smooth sea, with a fair wind. Lal remembers the hot sun, the awning rigged up aft for her, the pleasant seat that Captain Holstius arranged for her, where she lay listening to the plash of the water against the ship's side, rolling easily with the long waves of the Pacific, watching the white sails filled out, while the morning passed slowly on, marked by the striking of the bells.

It seemed, day after day, as her eye lay upon the broad stretch of waters, that they were quite alone in the world ; all the rest was a dream ; the creation meant nothing but a boundless ocean, and a single ship sailing slowly across it.

In the evening, after sunset, the stars came out—stars she had never seen before. They are no brighter, these stars of the equator, than those of the North. They are not so bright ; but, seen in the cloudless sky from the deck of the ship, they seemed brighter, clearer, nearer. Under their light, in the silence of the night, the girl's heart was lifted, while her companion stood beside her and spoke, out of his own fulness, noble thoughts about great deeds. She felt humbled, yet not lowered. She had never known this man before ; she never suspected, while he sat grave and silent among the other Captains, how his brain was like a well undefiled, a spring of sweet water, charged with thoughts that only come to the best among us, and then only in times of meditation and solitude.

Thinking of those nights, she would now, but for the sake of Rex, fain be once more leaning over the taffrail, listening to the slow and measured words of this gentle Norweegee.

As for Dick, he knew perfectly what they left England for, and why they came aboard this ship. At night, when they got into warm latitudes, he lay coiled up on deck, for'ard ; all day long he stood in the bows, and gazed out to sea, looking for the land where they were cast ashore.

It matters little about the details of the voyage. The first land they made was Oahu, one of the Sandwich Islands. They put in at Honolulu and took in fresh provisions. Then they sailed again across a lonely stretch of ocean, where there are no islands, where they hailed no vessel, and where the ocean soundings are deepest.

Then they came into seas studded with groups of islands most beautiful to look upon. But they stayed not at any, and still Dick stood in the bows and kept his watch. Sometimes his face would light up as he saw, far away, low down in the horizon, a bank of land, which might have been a cloud. He would point to it, gaze patiently till he could make it out, and then, as it disappointed, would turn away and take no more interest in it.

If you look at a map you will perceive that there lies, north of New Guinea, a broad open sea, some two thousand miles long, and five or six hundred in breadth. The sea is shut in by a group of islands, great and small, on the south, and another group, all small, on the north. There are thousands of these islands. No one ever goes to them except missionaries, ships in the *bêche de mer* trade, and ' blackbirders.' On some of them are found beach-combers, men who make their way, no one knows how, from isle to isle, who are white by birth, but Polynesian in habits and customs, as ignorant as Pagans, as destitute of morals and culture as the savages among whom they live. They have long since imparted their own vices to the people, and, as a matter of course, learned the native vices. They are the men who have relapsed into barbarism. All over the world there are found such men; they live among the lands where civilised men have been, but where they do not live. On some of these islands are missionary stations with missionary ships.

It was among these islands that they expected to find their castaway, or at least to hear something of him. And first Captain Holstius put his helm up for Kusaie, where there is a station of the American mission.

Kusaie, besides being a missionary station, occupies a central situation among the Carolines; if you look at the map you will see that it is comparatively easy of access for the surrounding islands. Unfortunately, however, communication between is limited. In the harbour there lay the missionary schooner, and a brig trading in *bêche de mèr*. She had returned from a cruise among the western islands. However, she had heard nothing of any such white man living among the natives. Nor could the missionaries help. They knew of none who answered at all to the description of Rex. But there were many places where they were not permitted to land, the people being suspicious and jealous; and there were other places where traders had set the people against them so, that they were sullen and would give no information. There was a white man, more than one white man, living among the islands in the great atoll of Hogoleu. There was a white man who had lived for thirty years on Lugunor, and had a grown-up family of dusky sons and daughters. There were one or two more, but they were all old sailors, deserters at first, who had run away from their ships, and settled down to a life of ignoble ease under the warm tropical sun, doing nothing among the people who were contented to do nothing but to breathe the air and live their years and then die.

One of them, an old beach-comber of Kusaie, who knew as much as any man can know of this great archipelago, gave them advice. He said that it was very unlikely a castaway would be killed even by jealous or revengeful islanders. No doubt he was living with the natives, but the difficulty might be to get him away; that the temper of the people had been greatly altered for the worse by the piratical kidnapping of English, Chilian, and Spanish ships; and he warned them, wherever they landed, to go with the utmost show of confidence, and to conceal their arms, which they must, however, carry.

From Kusaie they sailed to Ponapé, where the American missionaries have another station. Here they stayed a day or two on shore, and were hospitably entertained by the good people of the station, their wives making much of Lal, and presenting her with all manner of strange fruit and flowers. Here the girl, for the first time, partly comprehended what beautiful places lie about this world of ours, and how one can never rightly comprehend the fulness of this earth which declareth everywhere the glory of its Maker. There are old mysterious buildings at Ponapé, the builders of which belong to a race long since extinct, their meaning as long since forgotten as the people who designed them. They stand among the woods, like the deserted cities and temples of Central America, a riddle insoluble. As Lal stood beside those mysterious buildings with an old missionary, he told her how, thousands of years before, there was a race of people among these islands who built great temples to their unknown gods, carved idols, and hewed the rock into massive shapes, and who then passed away into silence and oblivion, leaving a mystery behind them, whose secret no one will ever discover. Lal thought the man who told her this, the man who had spent contentedly fifty years in the endeavour to teach the savages, who now dwelt here, more marvellous and more to be admired than these mysterious remains, but then she was no archæologist.

Then with more good wishes, again they put out to sea.

They were now in the very heart of the Caroline Archipelago. Nearly every day brought them in sight of some island. Dick, the Malay, in the bows, would spring to his feet and gaze intently while the land slowly grew before them and assumed definite proportions. Then he would sit down again as if disappointed, and shake his head, taking no more interest in the place. But, indeed, they could not possibly have reached the island they sought. That must be much farther to the west, somewhere near the Pelew Islands.

'See, Lal,' said Captain Holstius for the hundredth time over the chart, 'if Rex was right as to the current and the wind, he may have landed at any one of the Uliea Islands, or on the Swedes, or perhaps the Philip Islands, but I cannot think that he drifted farther east. If he was wrong about the currents, which is not likely, he may be on one of the Pelews, or on one of the islands south of Yap. If he had landed on Yap itself, he would have been sent home in one of the Hamburg ships, long ago. Let us try them all.'

For many weeks they sailed upon those smooth and sunny waters, sending ashore at every islet, and learning nothing. Lapped in the soft airs of the Pacific, the ship sailed slowly, making from one island to another. Lal lay idly on the deck, saying to herself, as each land came in sight, ' Haply we may find him here.' But they did not find him, and so they sailed away, to make a fresh attempt.

Does it help to name the places where they touched? You may find them on the map.

They examined every islet of the little groups. They ventured within the great lagoon of Hogoleu, a hundred miles across, where an archipelago of islets lies in the shallow land-locked sea, clothed with forest. The people came off to visit them, paddling in canoes of sandal-wood; there were two or three ships put in for pearls and *bêche de mer*. Then they touched at the Enderby Islands, the Royalist Islands, the Swede Islands, and the Uliea Islands.

' Perhaps,' said Captain Holstius, as they sighted every one, ' he may have drifted here.'

But he had not.

To these far-off islands few ships ever come. Yet from time to time there appears the white sail of a trader or a missionary schooner, or the smoke of an English war-vessel. The people are mostly gentle and obliging, when they recognise that the ship does not come to carry them off as coolies. But to all enquiries there was but one answer— that they had no white man among them, unless it was some poor beach-comber living among them and one of themselves. They knew nothing of any boat. Worse than all, Dick shook his head at every place, and showed no interest in the enquiries they prosecuted.

A voyage in these seas is not without danger. They are shallow seas, where new reefs, new coral islands, and new shoals are continually being formed, so that where a hundred years ago was safe sailing, there are now rocks above the surface, and even islands. There are earthquakes too, and volcanic eruptions. There are islands where plantations and villages have been swallowed up in a moment, and their places taken by boiling lather; in the seas lurk great sharks, and by the shores are poisonous fish. The people are not everywhere gentle and trustful; they have learned the vices of Europe and the treacheries of white men. They have been known to surround a becalmed ship and massacre all on board. Yet Captain Holstius went among them undaunted and without fear. They did not offer him any injury, letting him come and go unmolested. Trust begets trust.

So they sailed from end to end of this great archipelago and heard no news of Rex.

Then their hearts began to fail them.

But always in the bows sat Dick, searching the distant horizon, and in his face there was the look of one who knows that he is near the place which he would find.

And one day, after many days' sailing—I think they had been out of San Francisco seventy-five days, they observed a strange thing.

Dick began to grow restless. He borrowed the captain's glasses and looked through them, though his own eyes were almost as good. He rambled up and down the deck continually, scanning the horizon.

'See,' cried Lal, 'he knows the air of this place; he has been here before. Is there no land in sight?'

'None.' He gave her the glass. 'I see the line of sea and the blue sky. There is no land in sight.'

Yet what was the meaning of that restlessness? By some sense unknown to those who have the usual five, the man who could neither hear or speak knew very well that he was near the place they had come so far to find.

Captain Holstius showed his companion their position upon the chart.

'We are upon the open sea,' he said. 'Here are the Uliea Isles two hundred miles and more from anywhere. A little more and we shall be outside the shallow seas, and in the deep water again. Lal, we have searched so far in vain. He is not in the Carolines, then where can he be?

Nothing is between us and the Pelews excepting this little shoal.

The charts are not always perfect. The little shoal, since the chart was laid down, had become an atoll, with its reef and its lagoon.

It was early morning, not long after sunrise.

While they were looking upon the chart, which they knew by heart, the Malay burst into the cabin and seized Lal by the hand. He dragged her upon the deck, his eyes flashing, his lips parted, and pointed with both hands to the horizon. Then he nodded his head and sat down on deck once more, imitating the action of one who paddles.

Lal saw nothing.

The captain followed with his glasses.

'Land ahead,' he said slowly, ' off the starboard bow.'

He gave her the glasses. She looked, made out the land, and then offered the glass to Dick, who shook his head, pointed, and nodded again.

' We have found the place,' cried Lal ; ' I know it is—I feel it is—Oh, Rex, Rex, if we should find you there ! '

As the ship drew nearer, the excitement of the Malay increased. It became certain now that he had recognised the place, of which nothing could be seen except a low line of rock with white water breaking over it.

The day was nearly calm, a breath of air gently floating the vessel forward ; presently the rock became clearly defined ; a low reef, of a horseshoe shape, surrounded, save for a narrow entrance, a large lagoon of perfectly smooth water ; within the lagoon were visible two, or perhaps three islands, low, and apparently with little other vegetation than the universal pandang, that beneficent palm of the rocks which wants nothing but a little coral sand to grow in, and provides the islanders with food, clothing, roofs for their huts, and sails for their canoes.

As soon as Dick saw the entrance to the lagoon he ran to the boats and made signs that they should lower and row to the land.

' Let him have his way,' said the captain ; ' he shall be our leader now. Let us not be too confident, Lal, my dear but I verily believe that we have found the place, and, perhaps, the man.'

They lowered the boat. The first to jump into her was the Malay, who seated himself in the bows and seized an oar. Then he made signs to his mistress that she should come too.

They lowered her, and she sat in the stern. Then the captain got in, and they pushed off.

' What do you say, Lal ? ' asked Holstius, looking at her anxiously.

' I am praying,' she replied, with tears in her eyes. ' And I am thinking, brother,' she laid her hand in his, ' how good a man you are, and what reward we can give you, and what Rex will say to you.'

' I need no reward,' he said, ' but to know and to feel that you are happy. You will tell Rex, my dear, that I have been your brother since he was lost. Nothing more, Lal, never anything else. That has been enough.'

She burst into tears.

' Oh! what shall I tell him about you? what shall I not tell him? Shall I in very truth be able to tell him anything—to speak to him again? Kiss me, before all these men, that they may know how much I love my brother, and how grateful I am, and how I pray that God will reward you out of His infinite love.'

She laid her hand on his while he stooped his head and kissed her forehead.

' Enough of me,' he said ; ' think now of Rex.'

By this time they were in the mouth of the lagoon. The boat passed over a bar of coral, some eight feet deep, and then the water grew deeper. In this beautiful and remote spot Lal was to find her lover. All the while the Malay looked first to the islands and then back at his mistress, his face wreathed with smiles, and his eyes flashing with excitement.

The sea in this lagoon was perfectly, wonderfully transparent. The flowers of the seaweeds, the fish, the great sea slugs—the *bêches de mer*—collected by so many trading vessels; the sharks moving lazily about the shallow water were as easily visible as if they were on land. This small land-locked sea was, apparently, about three miles in diameter, bounded on all sides by the ring of narrow rocks, and entered by one narrow mouth. The islets, which had been visible from the ship, were four in number. The largest one, of irregular shape, appeared to be about a mile and a half long, and perhaps a mile broad ; it was a low island, thinly set with the pandang, the screw palm, which will grow when nothing else can find moisture in the sandy soil ; there were no signs of habitation visible. The other three islands, separated from the larger one, and from each other, by narrow straits, were quite small, the largest not more than two or three acres in extent.

The place was perfectly quiet; no sign of life was seen or heard.

Dick pointed to the large island, which ran out a low bend of cape towards the entrance of the lagoon. His face was terribly in earnest, he laughed no longer ; he kept looking from the island to his mistress and back again. As they drew nearer, he held up his finger to command silence.

The men took short strokes, dipping their

oars silently, so that nothing was heard but the grating of the oars in the rowlocks.

On rounding the cape they found a narrow level beach of sand stretching back about a hundred feet. This was the same place where, five months before, Captain Wattles held his conference with the prisoner.

'Easy!' cried the captain.

The boat with her weigh on slowly moved on towards the shore. There seemed on the placid bosom of the lagoon to be no current and no tide, nor any motion of the waters. For no fringe of hanging seaweed lay upon the rocks, nor was there any belt of the flotsam which lies round the vexed shores where waves beat and winds roar. Strange, there was not even the gentle murmur of the washing wavelet, which is never still elsewhere on the calmest day.

All held their breaths and listened. The air was so still that Lal heard the breathing of the boat's crew ; the boat slowly moved on towards the shore. The Malay in the bows had shipped his oar and now sat like a wild creature waiting for the moment to spring.

'Hush!' It was Lal who held up her finger.

There was a sound of distant voices. The place was not, then, uninhabited.

The boat neared the shore. When it was but

two feet or so from the shelving bank, the Malay leaped out of the bows, alighting on hands and knees, and ran, waving his arms, towards the wood.

It was now three months since the offer of freedom was brought to Rex and refused on conditions so hard. So far the prediction of Captain Wattles was fulfilled ; no sail had crossed the sea within sight of the lonely island, no ship had touched there. It was likely, indeed, that the castaway would live and die there abandoned and forgotten. Rex kept the probability before his mind ; he remembered Robinson Crusoe's famous list of things for which he might be grateful; he was well ; the place was healthy ; there was food in sufficiency though rough ; and he was ·not alone, though perhaps that fact was not altogether a subject for gratitude.

The sun was yet in the forenoon, and Rex, inventor-general of the island, while perfecting a method of improving the fishing by means of nets made of the pandang fibre, was startled by the rush of twenty or thirty of the people, seizing clubs and spears, and shouting to each other.

The rush and the shout could mean but one thing—a ship in sight.

He sprang to his feet, hesitated, and then went with them.

He saw, at first, nothing but a boat close to

land, and a figure running swiftly across the sandy beach.

What they saw, from the boat, was a group of very ferocious natives, yelling to one another and brandishing weapons, intent, no doubt, to slay and destroy every mother's son. They were darker of hue than most Polynesians; they were tattooed all over; their noses and ears were pierced and stuck with bits of tortoise-shell for ornament; their abundant and raven-black hair was twisted in knots on the top of their heads.

And among them stood one with a long brown beard; he wore a hat made out of a palm-leaf; his feet were bare; his clothes were shreds and rags; his bare arms were tattooed like the islanders' arms; his hair was long and matted; his cheeks, his hands, arms, and feet were bronzed; he might have passed for a native but for his face and hair.

It was exactly what Captain Wattles had seen, but that the men were fiercer.

When they saw from the boat the white man, they grasped each other's hands.

'Courage, Lal,' said Captain Holstius. 'Courage and caution.'

When Rex, among the natives, saw and recognised Dick, his faithful servant, running to greet him and kissing his hand; when he saw the people suddenly stop their shouts, and gather curiously about their old friend, who had been kidnapped long before with their own brother, he stared about him as if in a dream.

Then Dick seized his master's hand and pointed.

A ship was standing off the mouth of the lagoon; a boat was on the beach; and in the boat—— But just then Captain Holstius leaped ashore, and a girl after him. And then—then—the girl followed the Malay and ran towards him with arms outstretched, crying:

'Rex! Rex!'

This must be a dream. Yet no dream would throw upon his breast the girl of whom he thought day and night, his love, his promised wife.

'Rex! Rex! Do you not know me? Have you forgotten?'

For a while, indeed, he could not speak. The thing stunned him.

In a single moment he remembered all the past; the long despair of the weary time, especially of the last three months; the dreadful prospect before him; the thought of the long years creeping slowly on, unmarked even by spring or autumn; the loneliness of his life; the gradual sinking deeper and deeper, unto the level of the poor fellows around him; living or dead no one would know about him; perhaps the girl he loved being deceived into marrying the liar and villain who had sat in the boat and offered him conditions of freedom—he remembered all these things. He remembered, too, how of late he had thought that there might come a time when it would be well to end everything by a plunge in the transparent waters of the lagoon. Two minutes of struggle and all would be over. Death seemed a long and conscious sleep. To sleep unconscious and without a waking, is nothing. To sleep conscious of repose, knowing that there will be no more trouble, is the imaginary haven of the suicide.

Then he roused himself and clasped her to his heart, crying :

'My darling! You have come to find me!'

But how to get away?

First, he took the ribbons from Lal's hat and from her neck, and presented them to the chief, saying a few words of friendship and greeting.

The finery pleased the man, and he tied it round his neck, saying that it was good. The Malay he knew, and Rex he knew, but this phenomenon in bright-coloured ribbons he did not understand. Could she, too, mean kidnapping?

Meantime the boat was lying close to the beach, and beside the bow stood Captain Holstius, motionless, waiting.

'Lal,' said Rex. 'Go quietly back to the

boat and get in. Take Dick and make him get into the boat with you. I will follow. Do nothing hurriedly. Show no signs of fear.'

She obeyed; the people made no attempt to oppose her return; Captain Holstius helped her into the boat. Unfortunately Dick did not obey. He stood on the beach waiting.

Then Rex began, still talking to the people, to walk slowly towards the boat. He was promising to bring them presents from the ship; he begged them to stay where they were, and not to crowd round the boat; he bade them remember the bad man who stole two of their brothers, and he promised them to find out where they were and bring them back. They listened, nodded, and answered that what he said was good.

When he neared the boat they stood irresolute, grasping the idea that they were going to lose the white man who had been among them so long.

I believe that he would have got off quietly, but for the zeal of Dick, who could not restrain his impatience, but sprang forward and caught his old master in his strong arms, and tried to carry him into the boat.

Then the islanders yelled and made for the beach all together.

No one but Lal could tell, afterwards, exactly what happened at this moment.

It was this. Two of the islanders, who were in advance of the rest, arrived at the beach just as Dick had dragged his master into the boat. Captain Holstius had pushed her off and was standing by the bows, up to his knees in water, on the point of leaping in. In a moment more they would have been in deep water.

The black fellows, seeing that they were too late, stayed their feet, and poised their spears, aiming them, in the blind rage of the moment, at the man they had received amongst themselves and treated hospitably—at Rex. But as the weapons left their hands, Captain Holstius sprang into the boat, and standing upright, with outstretched arms, received in his own breast the two spears which would have pierced the heart of Rex. The action, though so swift as to take but a moment, was as deliberate as if it had been determined upon all along.

Then all was over. Rex was safely seated in the stern beside his sweetheart ; Dick was crouching at his feet; the boat was in deep water; the men were rowing their hardest ; the savages were yelling on the beach ; and at Lal's feet lay, pale and bleeding, the man who had saved the life of her lover at the price of his own.

She laid his pale face in her lap ; she took his cold hands in her own ; she kissed his cold forehead, while from his breast there flowed the red blood of his life, given, like his labour and his substance, to her.

He was not yet quite dead, and presently he opened his eyes—those soft blue eyes which had so often rested upon her as if they were guarding and sheltering her in tenderness and pity. They were full of love now, and even of joy, for Lal had got back her lover.

'We have found him, Lal,' he murmured—'we have found him. You will be happy again—now—you have got your heart's desire.'

What could she say? How could she reply?

'Do not cry, Lal dear. What matters for me—if—only—you—are happy?'

They were his last words.

Presently he pressed her fingers; his head, upon her lap, fell over on one side; his breath ceased.

So Captain Holstius, alone among the three, redeemed his pledge. If Lal was happy, what more had he to pray for upon this earth; What mattered, as he said, for him?

At sundown that evening, when the ship was under weigh again and the reef of the lonely unknown atoll low on the horizon, they buried the Captain in the deep, while Rex read the Service of the Dead.

The blood of Captain Holstius must be laid to the charge of his rival; the blood of all the white men murdered on Polynesian shores must be laid to the charge of those who have visited the island in order to kidnap the people, and those who have gone among them only to teach them some of the civilisation out of which they have extracted nothing but its vices.

As regards this little islet, the people know, in some vague way, that they have had living among them a man who was superior to themselves, who taught them things, and showed them certain small arts, by which he improved their mode of life; if ever, which we hope may not be their fate, they fall in with the beach-combers of Fiji, Samoa, or Hawaii, they will easily perceive that Rex Armiger was not one of them. They will remember that he was a person of such great importance that two chiefs came to see him; one of them carried off two of their people, the other, with whom was a great princess, carried off their prisoner himself.

In a few years' time the story will become a myth. Some of the missionaries are great hands at collecting folk-lore. They will land here and will presently enquire among the people for legends and traditions of the past. They will hear how, long, long ago (many years ago), they had living among them a white person, whose proper sphere—by birth—was the broad heaven; how he stayed with them a long time (many moons); how one after the other white persons came to see him, both bad and good; for some kidnapped their people and took them away to be eaten alive; how at last a goddess, all in crimson, blue, and gold, came with a male deity and took away their guest, who had, meantime, taught them how to make clothes, roofs, and bread, out of the beneficent pandang; how the companion was killed in an unlucky scrimmage; and how they look forward for their return—some day.

The missionaries will write down this story and send it home; wise men will get hold of it, and discuss its meaning. They will be divided into two classes; those who see in it a legend of the sun-god, the princess being nothing but the moon, and her companion the morning star; the other class will see in the story a corruption of the history of Moses. Others, more learned, will compare this legend with others exactly like it in almost all lands. It is, for instance, the same as the tale of Guinevere returning for Arthur, and will quote examples from Afghanistan, Alaska, Tierra del Fuego, Borneo, the valleys of the Lebanon, Socotra, Central America, and the Faroe Isles.

Five weeks later Lal was married at San

Francisco. The merchant who lent her the schooner gave her a country house for her honeymoon.

'She ought,' said Rex, 'to have married the man who gave her himself, all his fortune, and his very life. I am ashamed that so good a man has been sacrificed for my sake.'

'No, sir,' said the Californian; 'not for your sake at all, but for hers. We may remember some words about laying down your life for your friends. Perhaps it is worth the sacrifice of a life to have done so good and great a thing. If there were many more such men in the world, we might shortly expect to see the gates of Eden open again.'

'Unfortunately,' said Rex, 'there are more like Captain Wattles.'

'Yes, sir; I am sorry he is an American. But you can boast your Borlinder, who is, I believe, an Englishman.'

The account of Lal's return and the death of Captain Holstius duly appeared in the San Francisco papers. It was accompanied by strictures of some severity upon the conduct of Captain Barnabas B. Wattles, who was compared to the skunk of his native country.

It was this account, with these strictures, which the Son of Consolation found in the paper after posting his packet of lies.

Further, a Sydney paper asked if the Captain Barnabas B. Wattles, of the 'Fair Maria,' was the same Captain Wattles who behaved in the wonderful manner described in the Californian papers.

He wrote to say he was not.

From further information received, it presently appeared to everybody that he was that person.

He has now lost his ship, and I know not where he is nor what occupation he is at present following.

It remains only to suggest, rather than to describe, the joyful return to Seven Houses. We may not linger to relate how Mrs. Rydquist, who still found comfort in wearing additional crape to her widow's weeds for Rex, now kept it on for Captain Holstius, calling everybody's attention to the wonderful accuracy of her predictions: how Captain Zachariasen first sang a Nunc dimittis, loudly proclaiming his willingness to go since Lal was happy again; and then explained, lest he might be taken at his word, that perhaps it would be well to remain in order to experience the fulness of wisdom which comes with ninety years. He also takes great credit to himself for the able reading he had given of the mummicking.

The morning after their arrival, Rex, looking

for his wife, found her in the kitchen, making the pudding with her old bib on, and her white arms flecked with flour, just as he remembered her three years before. Beside her, the Patriarch slept in the wooden chair.

'It is all exactly the same,' he said ; 'yet with what a difference? And I have had three years of the kabobo. Lal, you are going to begin again the old housekeeping ? '

She shook her head and laughed, Then the tears came into her eyes.

'The Captains like this pudding,' she said. 'Let me please them once more, Rex, while I stand here looking through the window, at the trees in the churchyard and through the open door into the garden, and when I listen to the noise of the docks and the river, and for the white sails beyond the church, and watch the dear old man asleep there beside the fire, I cannot believe but that I shall hear another step, and turn round and see beside me, with his grave smile and tender eyes, Captain Holstius, standing as he used to stand in the doorway, watching me without a word.'

Rex kissed her. He could hear this talk without jealousy or pain. Yet it will always seem to him somehow, as if his wife has missed a better husband than himself, a feeling which may be useful in keeping down pride, vain conceit, and over masterfulness; vices which mar the conjugal happiness of many.

'He could never have been my husband,' the young wife went on in her happiness, thinking she spoke the whole truth; 'not even if I had never known you.   But I loved him, Rex.'

'LET NOTHING YOU DISMAY'

CHAPTER I.

WHEN the sun rose over northern England on a certain Sunday early in May—year of grace 1764 —it was exactly four o'clock in the morning. As regards the coast of Northumberland, he sprang with a leap out of a perfectly smooth sea into a perfectly cloudless sky, and if there were, as generally happens, certain fogs, mists, clouds, and vapours lying about the moors and fells among the Cheviots, they were too far from the town of Warkworth for its people to see them. The long cold spring was over at last ; the wallflower on the castle wall was in blossom ; the pale primroses had not yet all gone ; the lilac was preparing to throw out its blossoms ; the cuckoo was abroad ; the swallows were returning wtth tumultuous rush, as if they had had quite enough of the sunny south, and longed again for the battlements of the castle and the banks of Coquet ; the woods were full of song ; the nests were full of young

birds, chirping together, partly because they were
always hungry, partly because they were rejoicing
in the sunshine, and all the living creatures in
wood and field and river were hurrying, flying,
creeping, crawling, swimming, running, with
intent to eat each other out of house and home.

The eye of the sun fell upon empty streets
and closed houses—not even a poacher, much less
a thief or burglar, visible in the whole of Northumberland; and if there might be here and
there a gipsies' tent, the virtuous toes of the
occupants peeped out from beneath the canvas,
with never a thought of snaring hares or stealing
poultry. Even in Newcastle, which, if you come
to think of it, is pretty well for wickedness, the
night-watchmen slept in their boxes, lanterns long
since extinguished, and the wretches who had no
beds, no money, and slender hopes for the next
day's food, slept on the bunks and stalls about the
market. Nothing stirred except the hands of the
church clocks; and these moved steadily; the
quarters and the hour were struck. But for the
clocks, the towns might have been so many cities
of the dead, each house a tomb, each bed a silent
grave. The Northumbrian folk began to get up—
a little later than usual because it was Sunday—
first in the villages and farmhouses, next in the
small towns; last and latest, in Newcastle, which
was ever a lie-abed city.

Warkworth is quite a small town, and a great way from Newcastle. Therefore the people began to get up and dress about five. There were several reasons which justified them in being so early. Even on Sunday morning pigs and poultry have to be fed, cows to be milked, and horses to be groomed. Then there is the delightful feeling, peculiar to Sunday morning, that the earlier you get up, the longer you may lean with your shoulder against the door-post. Some men, on Sundays and holy-days, like to lie at full-length upon the grass, and gaze into the depths of the sky, till thirst impels them to rise and seek solace of beer. Some love to turn them in their beds as a door turneth upon its hinges; some delight to sit upon a rail; but the true Northumbrian loveth to stand with his shoulder hitched against a door-post. The attitude is one which brings repose to brain and body.

There is only one street in Warkworth. At one end of it is the church, and at the other end is the castle. The street runs uphill from church to castle. In the year 1764, the castle was more ruinous than it showed in later years, because the keep itself stood roofless, its stairs broken, and its floors fallen in—a great shell, echoing thunderously with all the winds. As for the walls, the ruined gateways, the foundations of the chapel, the yawning vaults, and the gutted towers, they have always been the same since the destruction of the place. The wallflowers and long grasses grew upon the broken battlements; blackberries and elder-bushes occupied the moat; the boys climbed up to perilous places by fragments of broken steps; the swallows flew about the lofty keep; the green woods hung upon the slopes above the river, and the winding Coquet rolled around the hill on which the castle stood—a solitary and deserted place. Yet in the evening there was one corner in which the light of a fire could always be seen. It came from a chamber beside the great gateway—that which looks upon the meadows to the south. Here lived the Fugleman. He had fitted a small window in the wall, constructed a door, built up the broken stones, and constituted himself, without asking leave of my Lord of Northumberland, sole tenant of Warkworth Castle.

I think there has always been about the same number of people and houses in Warkworth. If you reflect for a moment you will perceive that this must be so, partly because there is no room for any more on the river-washed peninsula upon which the town is built, and partly because while the same trades are practised for the same portion of country there must be the same number of craftsmen, and no more. You may expect, for instance, in every town, a shop where you can buy all the things which you must have yet cannot make for yourself, such as sugar, treacle, tape, cotton stuffs, flannel, needles, and thread. In country towns the number of things which can be made at home—and well made too—is more than dwellers where there are shops for everything would understand. In Warkworth, for example, there is a blacksmith—a man of substance, because everybody wants him and would pay him well; there is a carpenter and wheelwright, also a man to be respected, not only for his honourable craft, but also for the fields and meadows which he has bought; a tailor—but he is a starveling, because most people in Northumberland repair, if they do not make, at home; a cobbler, who has two apprentices and keeps both at work, because nobody but a cobbler can get inside a boot, to make or mend it; and a barber, who also has two apprentices. There is no baker, because all the bread is baked at home, which is one, among many reasons, why country life in this eighteenth century is so delightful; there is no brewer, because everybody, down to the cottager, brews his own beer—the old stingo, the humming October, and the small beer for the maids and children. Yet, for the sake of companionship, conversation, song, and the arrangement of matches, there must be an ale-house, with a settle round three sides of the room and another out-

side ; and for the quality there must be an inn.
There need be no place for the buying and selling
of butter, eggs, milk, or cream, because people
who have no cows are fain to go without these
luxuries, or else to beg and borrow. There need
be no butcher, because the farmers kill and send
word to the gentry when beef or mutton may be
had. There is no apothecary, because every
woman in the parish knows what are the best
simples for any complaint and where to find them.
There is no bookseller, because nobody at Warkworth ever wanted to read at all, and very few
know how ; one excepts the Vicar—who may read
the Fathers in Greek and Latin—and his Worship
Mr. Cuthbert Carnaby, Justice of the Peace, who
reads 'The Gentleman's Magazine,' to which he
once contributed a description of Warkworth.
There is, in fact, a singular contempt for literature
in the town, and it is, I believe, a remarkable
Northumbrian characteristic. There are no under-
takers, because in this county people have grown
out of the habit of dying, so that except in Newcastle, where people fight and kill each other, the
trade can only be carried on at a loss ; and there
are no lawyers, because the townsfolk of Warkworth desire to have nothing to do with law, and
are only concerned with one of the many laws by
which good order is maintained in this realm of
England—that, namely, which forbids the landing

of Geneva and brandy on the banks of the Coquet without vexatious and tedious ceremonies, including payment of hard money. If you, who live in great towns, consider the trades, crafts, and mysteries by which men get a living in these latter days, you will presently understand that most of them are unnecessary for the simple life.

When the first comers had looked up the street and down the street, straight through and across each other, and examined the sky and inspected the horizon, and obtained all possible information about the weather, they gave each other the good-morning, and asked for opinions on the subject of hay. Then one by one they went back to their houses—which are of stone, having very small windows with bull's-eye glass in leaden casements, and red-tiled roofs—and presently came out bearing with them their breakfast, such as two or three kned-cakes, or a chunk of three weeks' old bread, or a slice of bread-and-dripping, or bread and fat pork, or a pewter platter of bread and beef even, with a great pewter mug of small ale. They consumed their breakfast side by side in good fellowship, standing on the cobblestones or leaning against the door-posts, taking time over it: first a mouthful and then a drink, then a period of reflection, then a remark, and then another mouthful. They mostly had the Northumbrian face, which I am told is the Norwegian face—an oval shape, with soft blue eyes; with the face goeth a gentle voice and a slow manner of speech. They are a folk born by nature with so deep a love of life that they desire nothing better than to stretch out and prolong the present. Time, who is an inexorable tyrant, will not allow so much as a single moment to be stretched. Yet, by dint of slow motion, slow speech, a steady clinging to old customs, never doing to-day anything different from what you did yesterday and the day before, always talking the same talk at the same times, so that every duty of each season has its formula, wearing the same clothes, eating the same food, sitting in the same place, and avoiding all temptation to change, it is quite astonishing how the semblance of sameness may be given to time so that the whole of life shall seem, at the end of it, nothing but one delightful moment stretched out and prolonged for three-score years and ten.

After breakfast, for two hours by the clock they fell to stroking of stubbly chins and to wondering when the barber would be ready. This could not be until stroke of nine at least, because he had to comb, dress, and powder first the Vicar's wig for Sunday. Heaven forbid that the Church should be put off with anything short of a wig newly combed and newly curled ! And next the wig of his Worship Cuthbert Carnaby,

Esquire, Justice of the Peace and second cousin to his lordship the Earl of Northumberland, newly succeeded to the title. When this was done the barber addressed himself to the chins and cheeks of the townsfolk, and this with such dexterity and despatch that before the church-bell began he had them all despatched and turned off. And then their countenances were glorious, and shone in the sun like unto the face of a mirror, and felt as smooth to the enamoured finger as the chin and cheek of a maid. Thus does Art improve and correct Nature. The savage who weareth beard knows not this delight.

It was a day on which something out of the common was to happen; a day on which expectation was on tiptoe; and when at ten o'clock the first stroke of the church-bell began, all the boys with one and the same design turned their steps—slowly at first, and as if the business did not greatly matter, yet should be seen into—towards the church-yard. They were all in Sunday best; their hair smooth, their hands white, their shoes brushed, and their stockings clean; they moved as if drawn by invisible ropes; as if they could not choose but go; and whereas on ordinary Sundays not a lad among them all entered the church till the very last toll of the bell, on this day they made straight for the porch at the first, and this, although they knew that if they once set foot within it, they must pass straight on without lingering, into the church, and so take their seats, and have half an hour longer to wait in silence and good-behaviour, with liability to discipline. For a rod is ever ready in church as well as at home, for the back of him who shows himself void of understanding. The Fugleman, who wielded that rod, was strong of arm; and no boy could call himself fortunate, or boast that he had escaped the scourge of folly till the service was fairly done.

As regards the girls, who were still in the houses, at the first stroke of the bell they, too, hastened to put the finishing touch, with a ribbon and a white handkerchief, to the Sunday frock. And then, a good half an hour before the time, which was truly wonderful, they, like the boys, hastened to the church. At the first stroke of the bell the men, too, proceeded to equip them with the Sunday church-going clothes, which were very nearly the same in all weathers, to wit, every man wore his wide horseman's coat, his long waistcoat with sleeves, his thick woollen stockings, and his shoes, with steel buckles or without, according to their station. Thus attired they turned their faces all to the same point of the compass, and heavily, yet with resolution and set purpose, rolled down the hill into the church-yard.

Out in the fields, and in the fair meadows, and down the riverside, and along the quiet country paths, and among the woods which hang above the winding of the Coquet, the sound of the bell quickened the steps of those who were leisurely making their way to church, so that every man put best foot for'ard, with a 'Hurry up, lad! Lose not this morning's sight! Be in time! Quick, laggard!' and so forth, each to the other; those who were on horseback broke into a trot, and laughed at those who were afoot; the old women cried, alas! for their age, by reason of which limbs are stiff and folks can go no faster than they may, and so they might be too late for the best part of the show; the old men cursed the rheumatism which stiffened their knees, and bent their hips, and took the spring out of feet which would fain be elastic still, wherefore they must perhaps lose the first or opening scene. And the boys and girls who were with them took hands, and instead of walking with the respectful slow step which should mark the Sabbath, broke away from the elders, and raced, with a whoop and a holla, across the grass, a scandal to the mild-eyed kine, who love the day to be hallowed and kept holy.

At Morwick Mill, Mistress Barbara Humble would not go to church, though her brother did. Nor would she let any other of the household go, neither her man nor her maid, nor the stranger, if any, that was within her gates; but at half-past ten of the clock she called them together, and read aloud the Penitential Psalms and the Commination Service.

The show, meantime, had begun. At the first stroke of the bell there walked forth from the vestry-room a little procession of two. First came a tall spare man of sixty or so, bearing before him a pike. He was himself as straight and erect as the pike he carried; he wore his best suit, very magnificent, for it was his old uniform kept for Sundays and holidays: that of a sergeant in the Fourteenth, or Berkshire, Regiment of Foot, namely, a black three-cornered hat, a scarlet coat, faced with yellow and with yellow cuffs, scarlet waistcoat and breeches, white gaiters and white cravat. On the hat was in silver the White Horse of his regiment, and the motto 'Nec aspera terrent.' He walked slowly down the aisle with the precision of a machine, and his face was remarkable, because he was on duty, for having no expression whatever. You cannot draw a face, or in any way present the effigy of a human face which shall say nothing; that is beyond the power of the rudest or the most skilled artist; but some men have acquired this power over their own faces—diplomatists or soldiers they are by trade. This man was a soldier. He was so good a soldier that he had been promoted, first to be corporal, then to be sergeant, and lastly to be Fugleman, whose place was in the front before the whole regiment, and whose duty it was to lead the exercises at the word of command with his pike. In his age and retirement he acted as the executive officer in all matters connected with the ecclesiastical and civic functions of the town, whether to lead the responses, to conduct a baptism, a funeral, or a wedding, to set a man in the stocks and to stand over him, to cane a boy for laughing in church, to put a vagrant in pillory and stand beside him; to tie up an offender to the cart-tail and give him five dozen; or, as in the present case, to wrap a lad in a white sheet, and remain with him while he did public penance for his fault. He was constable, clerk, and guardian of the peace.

The boy who followed him was a tall and lusty youth, past sixteen, who might very well have passed for eighteen; a boy with rosy cheeks, blue eyes, and brown hair; but his eyes were downcast, his cheek was flushed with shame because he was clad from head to foot in a long white sheet, and he was placed so clothed, for the space of half an hour, while the bells rang for service, in the church porch, and then to stand up before all the congregation to ask pardon of the people, and to repeat the Lord's Prayer aloud in token of repentance.

The porch of Warkworth Church is large and square, fifteen feet across, with a stone bench on either side. The boy was stationed within the porch on the eastern side, and close to the church-door, so that all those who passed in must needs behold him. At his left hand stood the Fugleman, pike grounded and head erect, looking straight before him, and saying nothing except at the beginning, when discipline for a moment gave way to friendship, and he murmured: 'Heart up, Master Ralph! What odds is a white sheet?'

Then he became rigid, and neither spake nor moved. As for the penitent, he tried to imitate the rigidity of his companion, but with poor success, for his mouth trembled, and his eyes sank, and his colour came and went as the people, all of whom he knew, passed him with reproachful or pitying gaze. The church and the porch and the churchyard were all eyes; he was himself a gigantic monument of shame.

When the boys walked—as slowly as they possibly could—through the porch, they grinned and nudged each other. But for the stern aspect of the Fugleman they would have laughed aloud and danced with joy. They had, however, to move on and take their places in the church, and those were few indeed who were so privileged as to command a view through the open doors of the porch and its occupants.

When the men of the village ranged themselves as in a small amphitheatre round the porch, the younger ones, in a hoarse whisper said each to his neighbour: 'Oho! ha! yah!' After which they remained gazing with mouth agape.

The three interjections are capable of many meanings, and may indicate a great variety of feeling. Here was a lad found out and convicted on the clearest evidence and confession : he had made fools of the whole town ; here he was before all, undergoing the sentence pronounced upon him by his Worship, Mr. Carnaby ; and a sentence so seldom pronounced as to make it an occasion for wonder ; and the offender was not a gipsy or a vagrom man, or one of themselves, but young Ralph Embleton of Morwick Mill; and the offence was not robbing, or pilfering, or cheating, or smuggling, or beating and striking, but quite an unusual and even a romantic kind of offence, for which there was no name even; and an offence not falling within any law. Therefore their faces were fixed in an immovable gaze, and their mouths remained wide-open—some twenty or thirty mouths in all—like unto fly-traps.

When the girls, for their part, walked through the porch they looked at the offender with eyes of pity, and one or two shed tears, because it seemed dreadful that this tall and handsome lad should be compelled to stand up before all in guise so shameful. Yet he had caused many to tremble in their beds. But the elder women stopped as they passed and wagged their heads with frowns, and said: 'Oh, dear, dear! . . . Alack and alas! . . . . Tut, tut! . . . . Fye for shame! . . . . This is the end of wickedness. . . . . Ah, hinneys! . . . . Oh! oh! . . . . Look you now. . . . . Heigh, laddie! did a body ever hear the like?' and so forth, with grateful rustle of skirts, and so virtuously into the church. A noble example, indeed, for their own boys. Better one such illustration of the punishment which overtakes offenders than fifty patterns of the peace and tranquillity in which the good man begins and ends his days. Yet we humans are so foolish and perverse that we sometimes find vice attractive and the ways of virtue monotonous, and give no heed even to the most dreadful examples.

Towards the close of the ringing there entered the church, walking majestically through the lane formed by the rustics, Mr. Cuthbert Carnaby, Justice of the Peace, with Madam his good lady. He was attired in a full wig and a purple coat with laced ruffles, laced cravat, a flowered silk waistcoat, and gold buckles in his shoes; in his hand he carried a heavy gold-headed stick, and under his arm he bore his laced hat ; his ample cheeks were red, and red was his double chin. Though his bearing was full of authority, his eyes were kind, and when he saw the boy standing in the porch he felt inclined to remit the remainder of the punishment.

'So, Ralph,' he said, stopping to admonish him, ' thy father was a worthy man ; he hath not lived to see this. But courage, boy, and do the like no more. Shame attends folly. Thou art young ; let this be a lesson. After punishment and repentance cometh forgiveness ; so cheer up, my lad.'

'Ralph,' said his wife, with a smile in her eyes and a frown on her brow, ' I could find it in my heart to flog thee soundly, but thou art punished enough. Ghosts indeed ! and not a maid would go past the castle after dark for fear of this boy ! Let us hear no more about ghosts.'

She shook her finger—they both shook their fingers—she adjusted her hoop, and entered the church. The boy's heart felt lighter ; Mr. Carnaby and Madam would forgive him. His Worship went on, bearing before him his gold-headed stick, and walked up the aisle to his pew, a large room within the chancel, provided with chairs and cushions, curtains to keep off the draught, and a fireplace for winter.

After Mr. Carnaby there walked into the porch a man dressed in good broadcloth with white stockings, and shoes with silver buckles. And his coat had silver buttons, which marked him for a man of substance. His cheeks were full and his face fiery, as if he was one who, although young, lived well, and his eyes were small and too close together, which made him look like a pig. It was Mathew Humble, Ralph's cousin and guardian.

At sight of him the boy's face flushed and his lips parted; but he restrained himself and said nothing, while the Fugleman gave him an admonitory nudge with his elbow.

The man looked at Ralph from top to toe, as if examining into the arrangements, and anxious to see that all was properly and scientifically carried out.

'Ta-ta-ta!' he said with an air of dissatisfaction. 'What is this? Call you this penance? Where is the candle? Did his Worship say nothing about the candle?'

'Nothing,' replied the Fugleman with shortness.

'He ought to have carried a candle. Dear me! this is irregular. This spoils all. But—— Ah!—bareheaded'—he stood as far back as the breadth of the porch would allow, so as to get the full effect and to observe the picture from the best point of view—'in a long white sheet! Ah! bareheaded and in a long white sheet! Oh, what a disgraceful day! These are things, Fugleman, which end in the gallows. For an Embleton, too! If the old man can see it what will he think of the boy to whom he left the mill? And to beg pardon'—he smacked his lips with satisfaction—'to beg pardon of the people! Ah, and to repeat the Lord's Prayer in the church—the Lord's Prayer—in the church aloud! the Lord's Prayer—in the church—aloud—before all the people! Ah! Dear me—dear me!'

He wagged his head, as if he could not tear himself away from the spectacle of so much degradation. Then he added with a smile of perfect satisfaction a detail which he had forgotten :

'Standing, too! The Lord's Prayer—in the church—aloud—before all the people—standing! This is a pretty beginning, Fugleman, for sixteen years.'

If the Lord's Prayer in itself were something to be ashamed of he could not have spoken with greater contempt. The boy, however, looking, straight up into the roof of the porch, made no answer nor seemed to hear.

The speaker held up both hands, shook his head, sighed, and slowly withdrew into the church.

Then there came down the street an old lady in a white cap, a white apron, a shawl, and black mittens, an old lady with a face lined all over, with kind soft eyes and white hair, but her face was troubled. Beside her walked a girl of twelve or thereabouts, dressed in white frock and straw hat trimmed with white ribbon, and white cotton mittens, and she was crying and sobbing.

'Thou mayest stand up in the church,' said the old lady, 'when he repeats the Lord's Prayer, but not beside him in the porch.'

'But I helped him,' she cried. 'Oh, I am as bad as he! I am worse, because I laughed at him and encouraged him.'

'But thou hast not been sentenced,' said the old lady. 'It is thy punishment, child—and a heavy one—to feel that Ralph bears thy shame and his own too.'

'I was on one side of the hedge when Dame Ridley dropped her basket,' the child went on, crying more bitterly. 'I was on one side and he was on the other. Oh! oh! oh! She said there were two ghosts—I was one.'

When they reached the porch the girl, at sight of the boy in the sheet, ran and threw her arms about his neck and kissed him, and cried loud enough for all within to hear:

'Oh, Ralph, Ralph, it is wicked of them!'

These words were heard all over the church,

and Mathew Humble sprang to his feet, as if demanding that the speaker should be carried off to instant execution for contempt of court. All eyes were turned upon his Worship's pew, and I know not what would have happened, because his periwig was seen to be agitated and the gold head of his stick appeared above the pew; but luckily just then the bells clashed all together, frightening the swallows about the tower so that they flew straight to the castle and stayed there, and the Vicar come out of the vestry and sat down in the reading-desk, and, as was his custom, surveyed his church and congregation for a few minutes before the service began.

It is an old church of Norman work in parts patched up and rebuilt from time to time by the Percies, but there are no monuments of them. The Vicar's eyes fell upon a plain whitewashed building, provided with rows of ancient and worm-eaten benches, worn black by many generations of worshippers. The choir and the music sat at the west end. In front of the chancel was a square space in which was set a long stool. While the Vicar waited the Fugleman marched up the aisle, followed by the boy in the sheet, and both sat on this stool of repentance. Then the Vicar rose—he was a benignant old man, with white hair —and began to read in a full and musical voice how sinners may repent and find forgiveness. But the people thought he meant his words to apply this morning especially and only to the boy in the sheet. This made them feel surprisingly virtuous and inclined to sing praises with a glad heart. So, too, with the lessons, one of which dealt with the fate of a wicked king. All the people looked at the boy in the sheet, and felt that, under another name, it was his own story told beforehand, prophetically; and when they stood up to sing in thanksgiving, their gratitude took the form of being glad that they were not upon the stool. When the Psalms were read the people paid unusual attention, letting the boy have the benefit of all the penitential utterances, but taking the joyous verses to themselves. And the Litany they regarded as composed, as well as read, exclusively for this convicted sinner. Among the elder ladies there was hope that the offended ghosts might— some at least—be present in the church and see this humiliation, which would not fail to dispose their ghostlinesses to a benevolent attitude, and even influence the weather.

It seemed to the boy as if that service never would end. To the congregation it seemed, on account of this unusual episode, as if there never had been a service so short and so exciting.

When the Commandments had been recited, Ralph almost expected to hear an additional one, ' Thou shalt not pretend to be a ghost,' and be called on to pray, all by himself, for an inclination of the heart to keep that injunction. But the Vicar threw away the opportunity and ended as usual with the tenth commandment.

He gave out the psalm, and retired to put on his black gown. The music—consisting of a violin, a violoncello, and a clarionet—struck up the tune, and the choir, among whom Ralph ought to have been, hemmed and cleared their voices. The Northumbrians, as is well known, have good voices and good ears. The tune was 'Warwick,' and the psalm was that which began :

> Lord, in the morning thou shalt hear
> My voice ascend to thee.

The boy trembled because the words seemed to refer to the part he was about to play. His own voice would, immediately, be ascending high, but all by itself. He saw the face of his cousin, Mathew Humble, fixed upon him with ill-concealed and malignant joy. Why did Mathew hate him with such a bitter hatred? Also he saw the face of the girl who had been his partner; her eyes were full of tears; and at sight of her grief his own eyes became humid.

He did not take any part at all in the hymn.

When it was finished, the Vicar stood in his pulpit waiting; his Worship stood up in his pew, his face turned towards the culprit; in his hand

his great gold-headed cane.   All the people stared
at the culprit with curious eyes, as boys stare at
one of their companions when he is about to be
flogged.   Just then the girl left her seat and
stepped deliberately up the aisle, and stood beside
the boy in the sheet.   And the congregation
murmured wonder.

The Fugleman touched the boy's shoulder and
brought his pike to 'tention.

'Say after me,' he said aloud.   Then to the
congregation he added : 'And all the people
standing.'

'I confess my fault,' he began.

'I confess my fault,' repeated boy and girl
together.

'And am heartily sorry, and do beg forgiveness.'

And then the Lord's Prayer.

The boy spoke out the words clearly and
boldly, and with his was heard the girl's voice as
well, but both were nearly drowned by the loud
voice of the Fugleman.

It was over then.   All sat down ; the girl
beside Ralph on the stool of repentance, and the
sermon began.

The sermon which the Vicar read had nothing
to do with the penance just performed ; it was a
learned discourse, which would be afterwards
published, showing the Divine origin of the Hier-

archy; it was stuffed full of references to the Fathers, and conviction was conveyed to hearers' hearts (in case the arguments were difficult to follow) by quotations of Greek in the original. His Worship fell fast asleep; all the men in the church followed his example; the boys pinched and kicked each other, safe from the Fugleman for once: the women and the girls alone kept their eyes open, because they had on their best things, and with fine clothes go good manners, and the feminine sex loveth above all things to feel well dressed and therefore compelled to be well behaved. Even the Fugleman allowed his eyelids to drop, but never relinquished his pike; and the girl, holding Ralph fast by the hand, wondered if they would ever, as long as they lived, these two, recover from the dreadful disgrace of that morning.

When the Vicar had drubbed the pulpit to the very end of his manuscript, and the service was over, the three stood up again and remained standing till the people were all gone.

'Come, lass,' said the Fugleman when the church was empty, 'we can all go now. Off with that rag, Master Ralph.'

He unbent; his face assumed a human expression; he laid down the pike.

'What odds, I say, is a white sheet? Why, think 'twas a show for the lads which they haven't had for many a year. And May nigh gone already, and never a man in the stocks yet, and the pillory rotting for want of custom, and never a thief flogged, nor a bear-baiting. If it 'twasn't for the cocks of a Sunday afternoon and the wrestling, there would have been nothing for the poor fellows but your ghosts to keep· 'em out of mischief. And, lad,' he pointed in the direction of the mill, 'your cousin means more mischief. It was him that laid the information before his Worship.'

'Oh!' said Ralph, clenching his fists.

'Aye, him it was, and his Worship thought it mean, but he was bound to take notice, for why says his Worship, " he can't let this boy frighten all the maids out of their silly senses. Yet, for his own cousin and his guardian——" that's what his Worship said.'

Oh!' Again Ralph clenched his fists.

'Should I, an old soldier, preach mutiny? Never. But seeing that your cousin is no rightful officer of yourn, nor yet commissioned to carry pike in your company, why I, for one——'

'What, Fugleman?'

'I, for one, if I was a well-grown boy, nigh upon seventeen, the next time he gave orders for another six dozen, or even three dozen, I would ask him if he was strong enough to tie up a mutineer.'

The boy nodded his head.

'Cousin thof he be,' continued the Fugleman, 'captain or lieutenant is he not.'

The boy had by this time divested himself of his sheet, and stood dressed in a long brown coat and plainly-cut waistcoat; he, too, wore silver buckles to his shoes, like his cousin, but not silver buttons; his hair was tied with a black ribbon, and his hat was plain, without lace or ornament.

When his adviser had finished, he walked slowly down the empty church, hand-in-hand with the girl.

In the porch he stopped, threw his arm round her neck, and kissed her twice.

'No one but you, Drusy,' he said, 'would have done it. I'll never forget it, never, as long as I live. Go home to Granny, my dear, and have your dinner.'

'And will you go home, too, Ralph?'

'Yes, I am going home. I've got to have a talk with Mathew Humble.'

Left alone in the church, the Fugleman sat down irreverently on the steps of the pulpit, and laughed aloud.

'Mathew Humble,' he said, 'is going to be astonished.'

END OF THE FIRST VOLUME.

Spottiswoode & Co., Printers, New-street Square, London.